THE MARRIAGE BROKER

The

Marriage Broker

based on the stories of SHULEM

THE SHADCHEN by TASHRAK

Adapted by Irving Meites

G. P. Putnam's Sons : New York

Contents

THE MARRIAGE BROKER

1

How I Became a Marriage Broker

I am a marriage broker—a *shadchen*. **My** business card reads:

MORRIS SHULEM
Modern Shadchen
Girls and Widows with $5,000 to $50,000
Doctors, Lawyers, Business Men
ALWAYS ON HAND

Do you want to know how I became a marriage broker, a *shadchen?* It was just plain blind *mazel*, like walking in a dark street, at night, and stepping on a roll of hundred-dollar bills; or like marrying a poor girl for love only, and before the honeymoon is over, you hear an uncle of hers died and left her a million.

But before I tell you how it actually happened that I,

Morris Shulem, became a *shadchen,* I must say it still puzzles me. Why, in this jet age, when you can go from New York to Los Angeles in less time than it used to take to go on a Sunday to Coney Island from my house on Rivington Street, are there still some people who need a man like me, a marriage broker?

You know, people can find Saks Fifth Avenue from any place, and these same people will travel the complicated New York subway system, such as leaving the upper Bronx on the Lexington Avenue subway to Grand Central Station. Then they know how to follow the green lights on the ceiling of the walls under the streets of New York to the crosstown shuttle to Times Square Station and catch a train to Thirty-fourth Street where there is Macy's and Gimbel's, but still some of these same people just don't know how to meet their next door neighbor.

When I first came to this country, I started as a pushcart peddler. I made a living all right until I got rheumatism in my right leg, and then I was unable to attend business anymore. For a while I tried being an outside salesman, but this meant carrying a heavy sample case. Companies did not want me as an inside salesman because I did not have a following. Times were bad and the only following a person had was bill collectors. I even tried insurance—but whom do you sell insurance to? Your friends, and they were like me—broke.

It went from bad to worse, and I was compelled to apply to the Preventive Charity Organization to help me out of my pinched condition. It is a wonderful institution, that Preventive Charity Organization.

"Yours is an emergency case," said the lady who took my application. "We shall attend to it early tomorrow."

So I went home and waited patiently. The next day I was visited by a young man who looked like a newly graduated doctor. He measured my head and ears and felt the bumps on my skull. I asked him what the Preventive Charity Organization is going to do for me. He said he is sent to me just for a phrenological observation.

Next day comes another gentleman, an older one. He stabbed me with a needle, drawing blood, and informed me that he was the third assistant bacteriologist of the P.C.O.

On the third day comes an old maid, who was a regular district attorney, and wore eyeglasses that were cracked in the center. She asked me and my wife Minnie many questions. She wanted to know if I had any drunkards or wife beaters in my family. I told her that I come from a very nice family, and so does my wife, and that my parents were one time well-to-do people and charitable. She listened and kept writing in a little book and then explained that her visit was for the purpose of making out a report for the Social Science Bureau of the P.C.O.

On the fourth comes the landlord, Mr. Twersky, and he told me and Minnie we must vacate and get out of the apartment within three days or he will have us dispossessed.

No sooner than Mr. Twersky left, another investigator from the P.C.O. arrives. This one had a camera in his hands, and he took my fingerprints, saying he represented the Identification Bureau of the P.C.O.

On the fifth day comes what seems to Minnie and me to be the real thing—a lady investigator. She informed us she had a college degree. Her lips were the thin blue type. Forty-five she'll never see again and her weight from overeating was straining the buttons of her man-style suit. As soon as she comes into my apartment she espied a pair of brass candlesticks standing in the corner on a shelf. The lady investigator grabbed the candlesticks and said, "Why don't you sell or pawn these?" I pleaded that my great grandmother used them to light the Sabbath candles and that we had the candlesticks in our family for generations. Next she opened a drawer in the sideboard, and finding some worn-out table cover, she said with a sneer, "With such luxuries in the house you have the nerve to ask for charity?" Finally she looked in the icebox, but that was empty.

Next day—it was the sixth—comes a nurse, a young and beautiful nurse. She announced that she is sent by the Child Welfare Bureau of the P.C.O. to teach us how to prepare baby's milk bottle and how to wash the nipple. The nurse was disappointed when Minnie told her that we have no babies in the house and that our youngest child was a boy of nine, who left for school without any breakfast. Her face showed such real sadness when she heard of our boy going without food that she promised she will report our case to the manager of the organization immediately and recommend quick action.

While the nurse was still talking to me and to Minnie, Mr. Twersky the landlord comes to our door. He looked angry, and was about to *mach a tzimis,* but seeing the nurse in her white uniform and noticing a baby's milk bottle in her hands, he turned his eyes suspiciously first at me, then at Minnie, and with the commencement of a smile inquired, "Is it a boy or a girl?"

The nurse introduced herself to Mr. Twersky and explained the situation, as much as she knew of it. Mr. Twersky began to *shmoos* with the nurse and soon forgot the purpose of his visit. I was at a disadvantage because I did not understand as much English as I do now. They had a long talk and I could see by Mr. Twersky's facial expressions that he liked this lady from the Child Welfare

Bureau of the P.C.O. I also knew our landlord was a bachelor.

The nurse promises to meet with our landlord the next day. And Twersky agrees to wait for his rental until she had an opportunity to see the President of the Preventive Charity Organization and would inform him of the result.

"Morris, our landlord is in love with her," my Minnie said to me after they left together. "If, and it could happen, he marries her, you will have a good reason for claiming a *shadchen* fee."

"Minnie, that's a good idea," I said. "You have a good business head on you."

The next day, as it was arranged, the landlord and the pretty nurse meet again in my apartment, and Minnie and I left them to talk in the parlor. After Mr. Twersky had gone, the nurse told us she persuaded him to give us a month's free rental.

About an hour after the good news our landlord returned. He said he just wanted to know what the young lady said about him.

My wife volunteered to answer, saying, "Oh! She spoke kindly of you and that you are a very fine gentleman."

"She did?" exclaimed Mr. Twersky, pushing a five-dollar bill into Minnie's hand.

It is the eighth day since my visit to the office of the Preventive Charity Organization when the nurse calls on us again, and my wife told her confidentially that our landlord thinks she is the most charming young lady he ever met.

I could not help but add, "He is a wealthy man, and charitable too."

The nurse smiled her sheepish smile and handed me a check from the Preventive Charity Organization for $20. Ten days later Mr. Twersky came to us all smiles, and said:

"My friends, congratulate me, wish me *mazel tov:* Miss Katz, the nurse from the P.C.O., and I are engaged and we hope to be married soon. You will have your rent free for an additional thirty days and besides here is a check for $200, this being your fee as *shadchen.* However, *boychakal,* at the end of next month you will have to move, because I will have to fix the apartment up for my *kalle* and me."

So there I was, with no help from the Preventive Charity Organization, no apartment, but a $200 earned *shadchen* fee, so . . .

And that is how I became a *shadchen.*

2

Killing Six Birds with One Stone

Love is blind, and so is this business of a marriage broker. As blind a game as pinochle or poker. Sometimes I work hard for weeks and nothing comes of it; sometimes I hit the target right at the first shot, and in one instance I kill six birds with one single stone.

Let me tell you how it happened.

I always enjoyed stopping in, whenever I had a chance, at Carol Gonefsky's "SANDWICH TO A 10 COURSE DELIGHTFUL DINNER COFFEE SHOP." In the winter, Carol's place gave me a chance to warm up, while in the hot summer the fans gave me a cooling lift.

Mrs. Gonefsky has helped her husband, who had died roughly about seven years ago, build a fine business. Carol, as she liked her clientele to refer to her, always seated her diners and at the same time took the cash at the cash register.

"Conditions," Mrs. Gonefsky told me confidentially one hot day while I was enjoying a glass of iced tea, "have changed. Offices and shops in this neighborhood are now working only five days, while my rent and salaries to help are more than double, and prices are sky high overhead. Mr. Shulem," she continued, "I like to make a business proposition to you. I furnish some good leads—both ladies and gentlemen—but I want a commission on all marriages that you close because of me."

I do not like this kind of an arrangement, and I tell Mrs. Gonefsky I must talk it over with my wife Minnie, which the minute I had said it I knew it was a mistake. Minnie always is interested in my making new contacts for my clients' list. Also there are times when a *shadchen* has a long pause between deals.

It was this same Mrs. Gonefsky who spoke to me about a very fine girl by the name of Sadie Zuker. Mrs. Gonefsky impresses me so much with Miss Zuker that I make it a point to come back the next day at coffee-break time to meet personally this young lady.

Miss Zuker was all that Carol Gonefsky said she was and I decided to put the young lady on my active list. I must explain. A marriage broker is firmly convinced that all marriages are conceived in heaven—but once in a while heaven gets a little busy so the *shadchen* helps out. Therefore I as a marriage broker had two lists—one, active, and two, inactive. I always worked and tried my best for my active-list clients, and to date, to tell the truth, I have been more often successful than not.

Sadie Zuker was a stenographer who worked for Baldwin and Kasofsky, the herring importers. She was a regular picture and looked like she walked out of a Fifth Avenue window. Money she didn't have much, perhaps just enough to furnish up a three-room apartment.

It happened at this time I knew a fellow who didn't care much for money, or at least he said so. He also said, if I should run across in my list something really unusual I should keep him in mind. Such a fellow was Seymour Klinkowstein.

He had what you call a bugle. It has been my experience that a fellow who goes around bragging about marrying for love only is the one gets the girl with the cash.

A regular client this Klinkowstein refused to be. However, I would maybe once or twice a year stop in at Dvorsky's Men's Clothing Store uptown and look at a suit or a coat and talk with Dvorsky's star salesman.

It was on just such a trip when I told Klinkowstein about Miss Zuker, and he said he would like to meet her, but only in style. He said he would meet her at Sekler's Zion Theatre, and handed me $4 and told me to buy two seats for the theater's current attraction, *Blind Love*. One ticket I was to deliver to the young lady and the other I was to bring to him. That is one of the accepted ways many young people, who haven't got their parents here, and live with strangers, make their first acquaintance, with a view to matrimony.

Now, you know that fresh Kleingelder, who sits in Sekler's box office and sells tickets. When I asked him if he can let me have a pair of orchestra $2 seats for $3.50, he made a face as if he wanted to swallow me. But he let me have two seats just the same, only in my carelessness I didn't notice that they were for two single seats in two different sections of the house. One was for E175 right, and the other was for Q204 left.

For the remaining fifty cents I bought a seat for myself in the family circle, for I wanted to see the results that meeting would bring.

I was sleepy and did not wake up until the end of the

first act, because the subject of the play *Blind Love* really did not interest me. Not until the audience began to applaud at intermission and call for the author to come out on the stage and make a speech, did I awake. I walked out in the lobby, for I was sure that Klinkowstein would take Sadie out for an ice-cream soda or some treat of that kind.

Now, just imagine my surprise when I saw Klinkowstein with a girl not Sadie, but quite a stranger to me, and he was treating her to a box of lemon drops. I looked around the other way and there I saw Sadie in company of two young men, and one of them was buying her a box of chocolates. My first impulse was to go over and call Klinkowstein's attention to the error, for then I understood right away that that *goneff* Kleingelder had played a dirty trick on me when he sold me the tickets. But on second thought, I decided to let things go as they are and trust to luck. It is no use to be a smarty when the cards are against you.

After the last act was over, I saw all of them go to Stark's Café, and my heart began to beat for joy. I was almost sure I got the biggest catch of the season.

Next morning, brief case and umbrella in hand, I went to see Klinkowstein at Dvorsky's Clothing Store, and I found him in a very happy mood.

"You are a fine fellow," he upbraided. "Why did you tell me she was a girl? She told me that she is a widow. But that doesn't matter much anyway. It is true that she is not as pretty as you described her to me, but she has more money than I expected. Two lodges paid her on the death-benefit clause for the death of her husband, and she has several thousand more in the bank."

I was so happy at the news I felt like going out in the street and having a dance with myself. I kept telling myself, Klinkowstein wasn't interested in money, but he sure jumped at the opportunity of real cash.

In the evening I dropped in to Sadie Zuker. She was shining like a *kalle,* and looked as pretty as the moon.

"Oh, he is a fine young man," she said, "but he is not a clothing salesman, as you told me; he is an electrician. It is funny how you *shadchens* like to juggle with the truth. At first I did not know which one of the two men who sat near me was mine, for there were two, one on each side of me, and both were trying to engage me in conversation. So I decided on the one who sat at my right. And now the other one begged me to introduce him to you, so that you may find a girl for him, too."

"With the greatest of pleasure," I answered.

And on the next week I had to attend three engagement parties, and I saw six young people enjoying the happiness of love.

Love is blind, sure, and Mrs. Gonefsky collected half of my fee.

3

The Girl in the Window

How business methods have changed since the time I first started!

It used to be, for instance, a clothing store had "pullers." These "pullers" would talk up the merchandise and always make a speech how cheap in price and how wonderful the quality of the merchandise was. If you just stopped for a look in a show window up would step out of nowhere a "puller," and before you know it he would give you a story something like this:

"How the boss stays in business, I don't know, he gives away his goods. It must be strictly volume. Strictly volume. Come in and I'll show you." And the next thing you know you are in the store, buying.

Today, some up-to-date merchants hire girls to sit in store windows demonstrating all sorts of goods and inventions.

It brings in business. Sure. And belive me, Shulem the *shadchen,* they give nothing away.

Recently I was sitting in my office on a Monday morning, facing the yard, thinking of ways of drumming up some business for myself, and I thought *shadchens* ought to do something like this:

For instance: I would get window space in a drugstore, furnish up a model of a cozy little dining room and have a pretty young girl fuss about the table, setting it in beautiful order and serving tasty-looking dishes. And all of a sudden the girl would turn her face to the people outside and exhibit a large sign, saying, "Such is married life."

A demonstration like this would settle the minds of thousands of young men who fear the *shadchen* like an executioner. They would see the pleasures of married life, the enjoyments of a real home and good cooking done by loving hands. And while they would stand looking at the girl in the window, she would exhibit another sign with the inscription, "Go and see Shulem the *shadchen.*"

I had this idea in my mind for a long time until I confide it to Shpachner, the druggist on our corner. I wanted to get acquainted with the details of how to get the girls for this purpose, and the cost of it and so on.

"It is a good idea," Shpachner tells me, "but you would have troubles, nothing but troubles, in getting the girls. Instead of going to you the young men would grab them right from the window. I am talking from experience."

I became interested, and asked him to tell me of his experience.

"It is nothing new," he answered. "If I engage a girl to demonstrate a fountain pen, or a new safety razor, I have to look for another in a few days. Young men fall in love with them, and give them life jobs."

So I gave up my scheme and thought no more of it.

Two weeks later a young man comes to me and, introducing himself as Barney Sheinker, says that he would like to talk business with me.

"Well," he started slowly, "once I passed Shpachner's drugstore and I saw a girl in the window exhibiting fountain pens. The pens were to be given away free to everyone who wanted them. First I hesitated, for I could not believe it to be true, but the looks of the girl were so honest, so innocent, that I ventured to go in and ask for a pen.

" 'The pen is free,' she said, 'but you will have to buy two dollars' worth of ink and fifty cents' worth of writing paper with it.' You think I backed out? No. Mr. Shulem, I assure you that if the girl would have asked me to buy a barrel of ink and a whole ton of writing paper I wouldn't have been able to resist the sweet way in which she asked me.

"Next day I went again to see her. She was standing in the same window demonstrating a silver tie holder. I came in and handed her twenty-five cents for the holder. She looked at me and recognized me from the day before, so she wanted to fasten the holder on me with her own hands. Suddenly, she looked up surprised and said: 'Why, mister, you wear a bow.'

"On the third day she was selling some tonic to make the hair grow. How I envied the baldheaded man standing and staring at her! I made a dash for the nearest barbershop and told the barber to shave off some of my hair right in the center of the crown, making a bald spot the size of a silver dollar. Then I went to the drugstore and asked for a fifty-cent bottle of the hair grower. 'Oh how do you do?' she greeted me, and she advised me to take three bottles for a dollar twenty-five. That was a special price for me, she said.

"On the fourth day she was selling a new sort of corset. Here I was at a loss, not knowing what to do. I was about to go away, but I felt that if I did not talk to the girl just for one day I'd feel miserable. So I made up my mind that no matter what happened, I must go in and buy a corset.

" 'How do you do?' she greeted me. 'It is so good to see you again. What size corset does your wife wear?'

"The question stunned me, and for a time I stood speechless. She bent over to me and, whispering, she said: 'It is all right, mister; stout women make the best wives. Is she forty-two or forty-four? That is the largest we have in stock, but I can have one made to order. A woman just ordered a corset size fifty-four.'

" 'It's not for my wife,' I said; 'it is for my sister.' At that she laughed, saying: 'Oh, I catch on. It is for a sweetheart. All young men who go to buy things of this sort for their sweethearts say it is for their sisters. But surely, she must be more than a sister to you. Well, what is her size?'

"I told her that I really had no sweetheart. 'Then go and ask your sister what size corset she wears,' and she winked at me in such a way that all my blood rushed to my face.

"And now, Mr. Shulem," he at last came to the point, "now nobody can help me but you. I cannot go and meet her again, for she will ask me about the corset, and I don't want to lie to her."

"It is all right," I said. "Leave it to me. I am going to see her today, and you come back here in the evening. I may have good news for you."

By the time I arrived at Shpachner's the girl was demonstrating a new cure for corns.

I went to the drugstore and looked around carefully to see whether Shpachner was in his store, and seeing that he was out, I went straight to the girl in the window.

"A young man was here yesterday to order a corset from you," I said. "He promised to come again, but when he had to attend to some business, he sent me with the order."

"Oh yes," she said smiling at me. "I remember that he was to come and let me know his sister's corset size."

"It is not for his sister, but for his sweetheart," I corrected. "He was too bashful to tell you that he has a sweetheart."

"I see now," she said. "And what is the size corset he wants for his sweetheart?"

"Just like yours," I answered, "just exactly."

"My size is twenty-four," she declared with pride, "and the cost is two fifty."

"All right," I said. "Here is the money, take the corset and wear it in good health."

"What do you mean?" she asked, very much surprised.

In a few words I told her the whole story, and that she was the object of the young man's affections.

"He is a very nice young man," she said blushing, "I noticed it the first time he came in. Tell him he can call on me this evening. I live in Kugel Court with my uncle, Mr. Tzimson."

A few days later I met Shpachner, the druggist. So he says to me:

"What do you think, Mr. Shulem? I have lost another demonstrator. Someone swiped the girl and married her. From now on I am going to employ only married women. They may not be as attractive as girls, but at least they are safe."

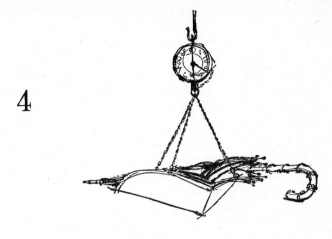

4

Sorkin the Buyer

The summer season just closed and New York was filled with buyers and lookers from all over the country. It is easy to tell the out-of-towners from the locals by the way they dress. The out-of-towners wear new shoes, new suits and new hats; all have fresh haircuts.

In this new fall season I happened to be on Broadway and Thirty-seventh Street and on the corner who should I meet but Mr. Adler, the manager of the Hospitality Hotel, and he says to me:

"Mr. Shulem, would you like to find a suitable party for a very nice young man from the South? If you would, you could make a nice couple of dollars."

"Such a question," said I, forgetting that Adler did not mention my sunburn that I worked hard all summer to get. "If I want to make a couple of dollars?" I continued, "especially if at the same time there is a chance to make two people happy."

"Any nice girl will be happy with Sorkin, buyer from Baum, Stein & O'Mally, general merchandise, of San Antonio, Texas," Adler said, reading from a card that he held in his hand. "He is here on business and, incidentally, he is looking for a match. It is hard for him, he says, to find a suitable party in his own town. So you'd better go see him, have a talk and start to hustle. He is in room 408."

I thanked Mr. Adler for the tip, and I made haste for the hotel to see Mr. Sorkin from San Antonio.

I found him in his room and I introduced myself by handing him my card. He looked and smiled, and then said:

"So you are a *shadchen!* And I suppose you have something to propose to me. I am very sorry, but you are too late. I have already met a party last night through another *shadchen,* and I think I am going to marry her."

"You a buyer for a big firm, and do you buy goods so quick?" I asked him in surprise. "Don't you see one brand of goods, then another, then another, until you get the best? And about such a thing as a wife you decide on first sight? So soon you make up your mind? Is it love at first *shadchen?* But New York is big, and there may be a prettier and better girl waiting for a chance to meet such a splendid young man as you. Anyhow, what harm can it be if you go and see another girl? Looking at goods does not mean giving an order."

"Perhaps, Mr. *Shadchen,* you are right," he said.

Seeing that he is about to give in, I asked him, "I wonder what is your idea of a good party?"

"Well, Mr. Shulem, sit down," he commenced, handing me a cigar. "Maybe, first, I'll give you an idea of myself, my background and my future, and I'll let you judge for yourself. I come from a good family, we are all in good health, I have a good education, and I have a good position. I am thirty-six years old, and earn $10,000 a year and have Texas real estate worth $30,000. I am not interested in money; the girl can be rich or poor, I don't care, but!"

To myself, I said, "Why does there always have to be a 'but.' "

"But!" Mr. Sorkin repeated, lighting a fresh cigar. "She must be educated, entertaining and pretty. This young lady that I am looking for must be very social. Let her be eighteen or even twenty-eight, it does not matter much, if only she meets with the other requirements, and she must be beautiful."

"I think I have on my list such a girl as you describe," I said, "and maybe fifty per cent better. If you don't want to go to see her I can arrange that I take lunch with her at Gonefsky's, and then you'll come over to our table and be introduced to her."

A real gleam came to his eyes when I described and told him of my client, but he wanted me to coax him a little before he gave in to meet her. As soon as I got an "all right, it's a deal, I'll meet your young lady," I was on my way. I went directly to the school where Minnie Shinkman was a schoolteacher. I waited for her to come out of school and asked to walk her home. On the way I told her about that buyer from San Antonio.

"Why," the schoolteacher said, quite irritated, "that is the same gentleman who Bercovich, the other *shadchen,* introduced to me last night!"

Can you picture to yourself how I felt when I heard that? Bercovich! I felt just like that *shlimazel* from my lodge who was expected to make a speech at our annual meeting, and he learned one by heart from a book of speeches. Then, when he came to the lodge he found that a man who was

to speak before him had learned the same speech. That is
how I felt when I discovered that Bercovich had nearly
finished this *shidduch* ahead of me.

"But wouldn't you like to see him again?" I pleaded, not
knowing how to get out of it.

"If I should want to see him again," she said, "I don't
need you to be my *shadchen*. But I never, never want to
see him again. Only last night he told me that at first sight
of me he felt that I am his destined one, and now he is trying to arrange a meeting with another girl, not knowing it
is the same one! How quick he changed his mind! He must
be one of those who are quick to fall in love and quick to
fall out of it. No, I don't want to see him again. Good day,
Mr. Shulem."

Miss Shinkman slammed her front door so hard the
whole house shook.

As I started to leave, my conscience began to pinch me.
First, I was sorry that such a gentleman as Sorkin should
lose such a splendid girl through no fault of his. I also knew
that Bercovich would surely think I did it on purpose, to
get a *shidduch* from him, and he would try his best to get
even with me.

I went home and tried to drown my sorrows in tea and
listen to the *bubba monsis* my wife would tell me.

Two hours later comes a telegram. I still have it with me.
It reads:

MORRIS SHULEM   421 RIVINGTON
CANCEL ORDER   HAVE DECIDED KEEP GOODS
PREVIOUSLY ORDERED   HOPE NO INCON-
VENIENCE   SORKIN

I took the telegram and with it I rush straight to Miss
Shinkman. Here was a chance to take the blame off poor
Sorkin, who is a fine gentleman from the South.

"Here," I said to Miss Shinkman, "read this telegram. Every word of it is burning with the passion of love. And if your heart is made of ice it will melt away."

She read the telegram and to my surprise burst out laughing. "Such an idiot!" she said. "And he thinks he is so smart? He thinks he can treat me like buying some goods! No, I do not want to see him again. This is final. Mr. Shulem, good-by."

Walking dejectedly in the street I met Bercovich. I greeted him cordially, but he stared daggers at me, and I began to explain.

"Listen, you, Shulem," he cut me off as soon as I started to speak, "don't try to pull the sheep's skin over your wolfish self. I know everything. I know how you tried to take away business from me, under my very nose. It is of no use to excuse yourself; I have fixed it already. I just went over to Sorkin and told him that the girl you proposed to him was a married woman whose husband eloped with her cousin. And he sent you a telegram with a plain hint to keep away from him."

"But listen, Mr. Bercovich," I said, grabbing him by the lapels of his coat as he was about to turn away, "the girl that I wanted to introduce him to was the same Miss Shinkman. I didn't know she was your client. You see?"

Then I told him the whole story and how Miss Shinkman got angry, thinking Mr. Sorkin had kept her on a string while at the same time he was looking for a better match. And that even now, after I showed her his telegram, she refused to see him again.

"Shlimazel!" Bercovich yelled with rage. "What have you done to me? Oh, what have you done to me?"

I felt in my heart that he was right, but I could not help him.

31

5

Shulem's Rival

"Mr. Shulem, it's good to see you." Joe greeted me as I walked into Carol Gonefsky's Café and sometimes called a *Kibitzarnie.* "You'll never know how good it is for me to see you. I need help and only you can get me out of Bercovich's clutches."

"Wait, a minute." I stopped Joe, who is a real fine waiter for the café. "Let me understand your *tzoris* and maybe I can help, but please first some tea and *shtrudel,* then talk."

"Here is your tea and I brought you apple *shtrudel,* it's today's, the cherry is from yesterday," said Joe while he waited on me. "And that Bercovich, I tell you, he is a bluffer from Bluffland. Is he tricky! I first made his acquaintance last month," continued Joe. "He came in here —a man past the middle age, with a high collar and a black suit and hat. I knew he was a *shadchen,* sure. I could tell it the way he looked at me. I don't know why, but my heart began to *klop*. Maybe it was a kind of foresight; for the heart, people say is a good prophet.

"The man sat down at one of the tables and began to read the bill of fare. What is the use of his reading? I said to myself. Everything that's written on the menu is already a dead letter at this hour of the day. Chopped liver, fricassee, meat balls and boiled beef are all gone. For an entree there remains only herring, the only dish always ready to serve. Then I see the man put down the bill of fare on the table, so I go to him and I say, 'What do you wish, sir? Regular dinner?'

" 'Yes,' he said, 'dinner. What have you got for entree?'

" 'We have chopped liver, fricassee, meat balls, boiled beef and herring,' I said to him all in one breath.

" 'Well,' he said, 'let me have chopped liver.'

" 'I am sorry,' I said, 'but we are all out of chopped liver.'

" 'Then give me fricassee or meat balls,' he said, taking another look at the menu.

" 'I regret,' I said, 'but we neither have left any fricassee nor meat balls.'

" 'And what about boiled beef?' he asked.

" 'We have only herring,' I answered him, but he was not satisfied, and he made a kick.

" 'Then why do you go into all that trouble and recite to me the whole list? Why didn't you say right at the start that you have only herring?'

"I explained to him that it was the ethics of my profession, first to offer the whole list of dishes and then serve whatever there was left in the kitchen. 'You see,' I say to him, 'that is the way we advertise business. If you can't get chopped liver today you will come for it tomorrow.'

" 'Well, let me have herring,' the *shadchen* said, and I saw my explanation satisfied him.

" 'After all, it was foolish of me not to order herring at first,' he said. 'It is, after all, the best appetizer. People are blind. I tell you—I am speaking of my experience in my own profession, as a *shadchen*. People as a rule never see the right thing at the start, but they first try to get those things which they cannot reach, and then they come back to plain herring. It is human nature, you know, and who knows human nature better than a *shadchen?*'

" 'And a waiter,' I added, for I won't let anybody cheat me out of credit.

" 'By the way,' said this *shadchen* when he got through with the herring, 'would you like to meet some nice party? I have a number of fine girls and young widows, with or without money. Let me read for you from the list in my notebook, and you tell me which you like best.'

"Here are six of the parties which the *shadchen* offered me. I put them on paper from memory.

"Party No. 10,741. A beautiful girl of nineteen, deaf and dumb. Wealthy parents would give $15,000 to worthy young man earning a fair and honest living.

"Party No. 10,742. Saleslady in millinery shop, age thirty-five; $800 in bank; not pretty, but willing to keep up her job after marriage or help husband in business.

"Party No. 10,743. Middle-aged widow; owns big corner grocery store; wants husband who could drive a delivery wagon.

"Party No. 10,744. Stenographer, seventeen, pretty as a doll, seeks party earning a fair living and who would marry her for her beauty only.

"Party No. 10,745. Good-looking, healthy girl, twenty-seven; worked as a cook in the best families; $1,200 in bank; a very good match for a practical young man.

"Party No. 10,746. Plain-looking girl, thirty-six, maybe

a little more; weight 230; comes from a family of rabbis; no money.

"After he got through reading the list he told me to pick my choice.

" 'Let me have the first one,' I said, 'the one with the $15,000.'

" 'I am very sorry,' he answered, 'but that girl married already last week.'

" 'Then let me have that saleslady with the $800,' I said.

" 'Why, how unfortunate!' and he shook his head. 'That saleslady is already engaged. She'll be married next month.'

" 'Well,' I said then, 'I think I could drive a delivery wagon for that widow with the corner grocery store.'

" 'Poor woman,' the *shadchen* almost cried, 'she died about a year ago. She was a fine woman, too.'

" 'Then I wouldn't mind to be introduced to that pretty stenographer,' I said.

" 'You are a smart fellow!' he complimented me and gave me a slap on my back. 'A beautiful girl like that is better than ten million dollars. It is too bad that she's married already and a mother of two kids.'

" 'And to make it short, that cook—poor girl! She lost all her money that she had in the bank. A young fellow, a swindler, made love to her, and thinking he was going to marry her she gave him the money to buy a candy store. So that *goneff* took the money and disappeared.'

" 'For you, Joe, is left that party No. 10,746. It is true, she is not a beauty and not a kid any more, and maybe a little bit heavy, but—take it from me—that is the kind of a girl that makes a good, faithful wife—not a flirt and not a loafer. She's a herring, true, but isn't herring the best thing, after all?'

"Well, he got even with me all right!

"It seems to me that there should be ethics in the profession of a *shadchen*, too, no Mr. Shulem?" Joe continued. "First, you got to read the whole catalogue and then try to dispose of what you have in stock. It advertises goods. But this *shadchen* made me promise to come with him some Sunday and meet his herring—that is, party No. 10,746. Another glass of tea and more *shtrudel*, did you say? All right, Mr. Shulem. Now I will continue my story—here is a slice of lemon for your tea.

"Did I go to see that party—No. 10,746? You bet I did. I had to. Bercovich the *shadchen* stuck to me like molasses and would not let me off. He came here Sunday noon just as I was going to leave the café for my afternoon off, and said: 'They are expecting you over there this evening.'

" 'Who is expecting me?' I asked him, for, to tell the truth, I forgot all about the *shidduch* he had offered me.

" 'Why,' he said, taking out the same notebook that he had with him last time, and he read to me: 'Party No. 10,746. Plain-looking girl, thirty-six, maybe a little older, weight 230; comes from a good religious family; no money. This is the party you wanted to meet. Now I made an appointment for you to meet her at her mother's house at half-past seven this evening. Please be a gentleman; don't disappoint her. It's worth while to meet such a girl for she is a regular jewel, a diamond; may you have such luck!'

"So I promised him to be there on time.

"In the evening I put on my holiday suit and a tie that was once given to me by a customer whose wife objected to its color, and I went to meet the young lady, whose name was Perele Klotz.

"After climbing four flights of stairs I was told that I was in the wrong house, and that 314 Rivington Street was the next house, on the right side. So I climbed another flight of stairs to the roof, and from there I crossed over to the next building, on the right, and soon I found myself facing Miss Klotz's mother.

"The old lady who met me at the door gave me a cordial 'How do you do?' and she led me to the parlor. 'My Perele will come in right away,' she said to me. 'You know, all the pretty girls like to look still prettier. Oh, she is such a darling, my Perele; a real pearl! So good, so devoted—she'll make a husband happy. She is not like other girls who go around flirting with every boy they meet. And that is maybe the reason she is still with her mother. But I am sure her destined one will come and that he'll be one that is worthy of her. Excuse me, I'll be back soon.'

"On the table I saw a big spread in my honor. But I was more interested in the conversation between Perele and her ma. I have good ears and I could hear it—nearly every word of it.

"'Try and be smart, my daughter,' I heard the mother say. 'He seems to be a fine boy. That's right, Perele. Put some more of that stuff on your other cheek. Maybe he'll fall in love with you. It is about time for you to get a husband. What's the use of fooling around with that bald-headed barber, Gimpelson? You think it is a secret? Why, everybody in the block talks about it. Yossel, the janitor, saw him kiss you in the hall one night and he told everybody. I warned you a hundred thousand times to keep away from that loafer Gimpelson. He has a wife in Europe. I hope this young man who is here now will never hear of it, and I hope no enemy will tell him of the trouble that we had six months ago, when we lived in Fourth Street, when cross-eyed Yetta Solomon, the truckman's wife, traced you and her husband to a moving-picture theater, and there she made such a *gevalt* and a riot that we had to move from the neighborhood.'

"Of course, all that was very valuable information for me. But here, mother and daughter came in, and I was introduced to Perele. The *shadchen* did not exaggerate a bit. She was thirty-six, and maybe more, but she bore her 230 pounds with a light step, and her triple chin shook at every move she was making.

" 'My daughter is very pleased to meet you,' said the mother, who did all the talking. 'She wants you to sit down right by her, but she is too bashful to say it herself. Peel off an orange for him, Perele; don't be bashful.' Then turning to me, the mother said: 'I don't know why, but I liked you at first sight. I feel already as if you were my own son.'

"I sat there for half an hour or so. Then I told them I had an important letter to write, which must be dropped in the letter box before the last Sunday night collection, and, therefore, I must cut my visit short. The old lady invites me to call again.

"As soon as I came home I began to write the letter, addressing it to myself. Here it is, Mr. Shulem, let me read it to you:

"Mr. Joe Katzman: Don't be blind; look out! Don't believe a word of what that liar of a *shadchen*, Bercovich, is telling you. Perele Klotz is a girl I wouldn't wish my worst enemy for a wife. It is all a big bluff about the rabbis in her family. Six months ago she and her mother were compelled to move from Fourth Street, because a woman living in the neighborhood made a riot in a moving-picture place when she found her husband and Perele Klotz sitting together and eating peanuts from the same bag. In the block where the Klotz girl lives now there is a barber by the name of Gimpelson, who has a wife in Europe, but he likes Perele much better. They are on kissing terms.

"This letter I signed 'A Lover of Truth,' and I mailed

it the same night. Next morning the mailman brought it back to me. I opened it and read it again, and for great joy I shook hands with myself.

"So you know what I did? In the afternoon, when Bercovich the *shadchen* came to the restaurant to ask me about his party No. 10,746, I showed him the letter.

"Oh, you ought to see what a face he made! Believe me, I felt sorry for him, for, after all, he is struggling hard to make a living for his family. But he soon regained his courage and said:

" 'That rascal who wrote this is a liar, and he should die a horrible death tonight. I'm sure he was in love with that girl, but she turned him down. Maybe it was sent by some eugenic professor who wants to ruin my business. Don't you believe a word that he writes. You can see that the letter was written for spite. We all have our enemies, and we can't tell what they would say about us if they only could make people believe them.'

"Then the *shadchen* left, murmuring to himself, 'Such *shlimazel!* Such bad luck!'

"Did I do right, Mr. Shulem?" Joe concluded. "If I want a *shidduch* you'll find me one. But I don't want a *shidduch;* I'm too tired."

6

Compatible

Sometimes, like any businessman, I run into slumps. Every *shidduch* I undertake proves a failure. August is the *shadchen's* slack season. One year expenses continued and still eleven days left in August and six more days till Labor Day, a total of seventeen days of *tzoris* for me.

With nothing going right, I decided maybe a change in procedure would do the trick. Always I take the man to the girl's house, where usually a nice table is set, and all the parties concerned are nicely dressed and the hopeful *kalle's* parents walk around like they are walking on eggs.

This young man I have in mind is a *fresser;* he eats and eats and eats. He attacks plates of food and sweets. When he is about sixty per cent finished with all the food on the table, and I am good and embarrassed, he'll say in a voice that can be heard across the street, "I don't like her, so let's go."

After about three of these situations, the only reason I am sticking with this client is I promised his father, on his father's deathbed, I would get Robert married to a nice girl from a good family. Robert's father left him a nice income that comes every month from the insurance company, so money he doesn't need. But when I would bring him to a girl for an introduction, he would eat and act in such a way, I would lose the girl as a client.

As I say, August is bad, so finally I decided to have a talk with Robert's mother. Since they live in a big house overlooking Central Park, I figured it would be nice, just for a change, to bring a girl and her parents to the Levins' and let Mrs. Levin put on the spread. When Robert heard this he became excited and kept hollering, "No, no, no."

I said to him, "What do you want in a girl? Give me an idea? You must be married sooner or later."

"I've got plenty of time yet," was his answer. "First I want to see if the girl and I are compatible."

"*Oy*," I said to myself. I don't have enough trouble with August, now I've got "compatible." I wouldn't ask Robert what it meant, because he said it in front of his mother, so I felt it couldn't be bad. "I'll look into it, and you'll have an answer by five o'clock tomorrow afternoon, good-by," and I gladly left. Believe me, under any other circumstances I would have walked away completely, but I made a promise to a dying man. And business was slow.

When I came home Benchy, my grandson, was playing a game of domino with his grandmother and I felt I was finally getting a little bit of *mazel*. "Benchy," I proudly called to my grandson, "you are a smart boy, you get B plus and a couple of A's on your report card, tell me what does 'compatible' mean."

If you ever saw a blank look in your life, it could not possibly match Benchy's. "I don't know, Grampa, and I've got to go home right now, good-by," said Benchy, and he was on his way.

"Wait a minute," I said, grabbing him gently by the arm.

"I don't know the word," protested Benchy, "I never heard the word in my whole life! But I'll tell you what. Tomorrow, I will ask Miss Smith in the library, and then I'll tell you, good-by." And off he went.

"Come right here after library," I called after my grandson, "and let me know."

Benchy, who is always prompt, did not arrive until a quarter of five the next day. Before the boy had a chance to say a word, I shouted, "Where were you? Playing baseball?" I was annoyed because I had my appointment in fifteen minutes. "Hurry, tell me what is this 'compatible?' "

"I'm late because of that word," was Benchy's answer. "Miss Smith made me put back on the shelf a hundred books."

"*Nu*," my patience was almost at an end, "so what does it mean?"

"Miss Smith asked me why I wanted to know," answered Benchy, "and I told her you were a *shadchen*, and a man wanted to be 'compatible' with a lady before he married her, so she turned red in the face and made me put the books away and gave me this note to give you. Here."

I ripped the envelope open and read: "Compatible, in regard to marriage, means, are two people suited for each other—like trial marriage, and you should not send your grandson to ask your questions. Please stop in at the library and perhaps you can find someone for me." It was signed Esther Smith.

"Oh! so that's the kind of a fellow Robert is? I'll fix his clock!" I said to myself as I left to go to the Levins'.

I arrive a little late, and explained to Mrs. Levin that

her Robert was trying to be a "wild" boy and also that I have a new prospect in mind for him, a librarian, who won't stand for any monkey business. "Please Mrs. Levin, give your son a good talking to, and don't forget to teach him manners."

"Don't you worry, Mr. Shulem," said Mrs. Levin, "my husband, may he rest in peace, and I gave you our thanks each time when you got for us four *chosons* for our four girls. I'll take care of my son."

I left and went straight to the library to see Miss Smith. She was a nice thin girl that wore glasses and a flat sweater and shoes. I had a nice talk with her and she invited me to come to her house and meet her father, the soda-water manufacturer.

It wasn't necessary for Mrs. Levin to put on a spread after all, for Mr. Smith, who changed his name from Schlepperman after he became a success, and his wife put on a regular banquet.

Mrs. Levin took care of her son by feeding him six big knockwursts before he left his house to go to the Smiths'.

Robert and Esther were married before the first of the year and they must be "compatible" because they read books together, eat together and do everything together, and Mr. Smith's nice-sized check for my *shadchen* fee made me "compatible" too.

7

A Romance of the Clothesline

Monday is a dull day for a man in my business. Monday mornings are a complete waste of time for a *shadchen*.

For those who are lucky enough to have parties or dates to attend on the weekend, Monday becomes a day of reflection. For those who did not go out, Monday is indeed a blue day, especially when others are overheard talking what they did on those two days previous.

So is it with me. Monday morning I usually stay home. I have a little private office in my house where I like to sit and meditate and look through the window which faces the yard. On Mondays, the yard with its many clotheslines looks very interesting to a *shadchen*. By the clothes on the lines I can tell exactly how many grownups there are in every family, and sometimes as I watch the linen dangling from the ropes I match in my thoughts blouses and shirts, stockings with socks. Having been a peddler some years ago, I know a little about the value of linen, and I try to make an estimate of the financial standing of the family whose clothes are hung out on the line to dry.

With time, this clotheslines watching became like a habit.

While sitting and meditating one Monday morning I became interested in a flat of the house to my left, No. 420. The clothes that the woman of that flat hung out every Monday told me she was a mother of five grown-up girls. The clothes also told me the girls were of the kind that have positions and are earning a good living. But I could not tell whether they had saved up for *nadan,* or they spent it all.

"Minnie," I ask my wife, "who is the woman with the five girls that lives next door?"

"That is Mrs. Steinberg, a widow, with five daughters," my wife informs me. "They are fine girls, nice-looking, and are making money. The oldest is a schoolteacher, one is a piano teacher and three work in offices. But why do you ask?"

"Oh, just so," I said, for I have learned by experience it is best to tell my wife as little as is necessary about my plans. Big decisions when I have to make, I always discuss with Minnie. But little ones, women have a way of splashing ice water on a man's ambitions, and it is best I keep my mouth shut.

And then I commence to think hard of a way to get the right kind of boys for the five daughters of Mrs. Steinberg.

One day a new family moved in the house, No. 422, next to the house in which Mrs. Steinberg lived. On the first Monday after the new family moved in, I notice a woman hanging out linen on the lines. After she was through I knew she had five grown-up sons.

"*Gottinu!* I got it at last!" I said to myself. "The five boys of No. 422 will marry the five girls of No. 420. I must start to work right away."

Taking a good look at their linen, I could tell that the boys are sporty fellows, just the kind of young men for real American girls, as the Steinberg sisters are. Since then my thoughts were traveling back and forth from the house No. 420 to the house No. 422, and as I looked in the yard all I could see were the two particular clotheslines swing to and fro and flirting with each other.

Sometimes I would grow skeptical. Number 422 was an elevator apartment with all modern improvements, doorman and all, while No. 420 was just a house of flats, built for people of moderate means. People of elevator apartments and those who live in plain flat houses seldom get together.

But looking in the face of the woman of No. 422 while she was hanging out the clothes, I saw she was one of those old-fashioned motherly women, and I knew she would be happy to get for her sons real good girls like the Steinberg sisters.

So I began to think hard how to bring the two families together. Finally, I paid a visit to Mrs. Steinberg, of the house No. 420. Her daughters were not home, for it was only four in the afternoon. After introducing myself, I gave her a little talk about marrying off girls early, while they are still young and pretty and while they are willing to take a mother's advice.

Mrs. Steinberg agreed with me. "But," she said, "the trouble is that my girls have no money. All that is left of their earnings they spend on clothes. You know how girls have to dress nowadays."

"Yes, I know," tell her, "but the fine clothes help a *shadchen* a great deal. I have in mind five young men, brothers, real American boys who, I am sure, would like just the kind of girls you have."

"Five brothers marrying five sisters!" the woman exclaimed. "It sounds like a beautiful fairy tale; it's too good to be true."

"Well," I said, "if five brothers will not marry five sisters, maybe four will, maybe three or maybe two. And even if only one of the brothers will marry one of your girls, what can you lose by it? We shall see about the rest later."

Then I told her my scheme.

"Well, well," Mrs. Steinberg laughed, as she was cutting noodles, "you *shadchens* have brains. I saw that woman so often hang out her clothes on the line, but I never thought to find out whether she had boys or girls, and you know exactly that she has five boys? I guess every professional man becomes an expert in the long run."

Before I had a chance to go up and see the other party, the one of the elevator apartment house, there came a great stroke of *mazel*.

Monday, soon after the women hung out their wash in the yard, a heavy storm came, and then and there was a rush for the lines to take in the clothes. In the rush Mrs. Steinberg dropped two pairs of stockings, and they fell on the ground. Just as she came down in the yard to pick up the stockings, a man's shirt fell off the line of Mrs. Beresofsky, the woman who lived in the elevator apartment house and who had the five sons.

I saw Mrs. Steinberg pick up the shirt and go out through the yard into the street. I knew where she was going.

"As I rang her bell," Mrs. Steinberg relates to me five minutes later, "Mrs. Beresofsky came to meet me at the

door. She thanked me for bringing up the shirt and said
that she noticed me many times before. And when I asked
her to call on me with her children she accepted my invitation, saying that she considers it a great honor and will call
tonight!"

"With her sons?" I asked.

"Yes, with her sons," Mrs. Steinberg said. "Now I must
hurry and go to prepare some good things for the guests.
They're coming about half past eight in the evening."

All evening I was on pins and needles and when the clock
struck nine no longer could I stand it, so I went straight
to Mrs. Steinberg's house.

"Hush!" she said to me in a whisper, meeting me at the
door, "don't say a word and don't come in. As soon as
I get rid of them I'll come to your house and tell you."

Why? I could not understand why Mrs. Steinberg
wanted to get rid of her company so soon. It was a puzzle.

Two hours later comes Mrs. Steinberg to my house. She
was on the verge of collapse when she commences her
explanation:

"It was all a mistake, Mr. Shulem! The woman we saw
hang up the clothes from the window of the next-door
house is not Mrs. Beresofsky but the woman who is doing
Mrs. Beresofsky's washing, and it was this washwoman that
I invited to my house. *Oy!* She came with her eight—very
wild boys—and they ate up everything. The oldest, who is
only fourteen, ate a whole loaf of rye. Well, I am glad to
see them eat if they're so hungry, but the mother says she
will surely call again soon. *Oy,* Mr. Shulem, tell me, advise,
what am I to do?"

Now, what kind of advice could I give her?

8

A Pair of Socks

I don't remember exactly if it was Robinson Crusoe
that this happened to. At the time, Mr. Crusoe was ship-
wrecked and he just finished his last bottle of dill pickles.
So he wrote a note, stuffed it into the bottle which he tossed
out into the sea and hoped that he would be rescued. It
could be that I have the wrong party, but I have read of
such letters and that they brought good results.

About a year ago, when I took Minnie, my wife, for a
two weeks' stay in Tannersville, I bought a pair of socks
of one of the summer resort peddlers. It was an ordinary
forty-nine cent pair of socks, the kind you get in the city
two pairs for thirty-nine. When I tore off the paper band
that fastened the socks together a note fell out which read:

Please write to me.
BELLA GUTKIND,
4444 Pitkin Ave.,
Brownsville, New York

"Look here," I said to Minnie, my wife. "Here is a girl who wants me to write to her. Does she know me?"

"This is the way some girls try to get husbands," Minnie explained to me. "I suppose the girl is a packer in the factory where socks are made, and she slipped in the note, hoping it will reach some young man who will become interested in her."

"A strange way of getting a husband," I mused.

"Many girls do this, and some succeed."

"Well," I said, "I'm going to write to that Bella Gutkind anyhow. Her note fell in the hands of a reliable *shadchen*. She has *mazel*."

So I sat down and wrote:

Much Esteemed Miss Bella Gutkind:

I was very happy to find your note in a pair of socks that I bought today, and I thank you very much for your invitation to write to you. I shall be very glad to call on you if you will honor me with an appointment.

All I can say of myself at present is that I am a man of honor, no trifler, and that my intentions are honorable. The rest you will learn when we shall meet, which I hope will be very soon.

Most respectfully yours,
Morris Shulem,
Care Hotel Kugel, Tannersville.

Three days later comes her answer. It read something like this:

Dear Mr. Shulem:

I was so happy to receive your note, the friendly tone of which indicates that you are a man worth while knowing. My parents and I shall be delighted to see you at our house any day you come back from Tannersville.

I read your letter twenty times, and the more I read the more I liked it. Every word went straight to my heart, and I wish the time until I can see the author would fly.

Meanwhile please write to me, dear friend. Write every day, and if you can not write send me a picture postal card.

With ✕ (just one at present),

Bella

For the rest of the time that I stayed with Minnie in Tannersville, I mailed Bella a picture postal card every day. The day we returned home I wrote to Bella, asking her to expect me the next evening.

When I arrived at the house a middle-aged woman, who wore a black sateen dress, met me at the door.

"I want to see Miss Bella Gutkind," I said to the lady in the shiny dress.

"Bella! Bella!" the woman called to the parlor door. "Bella, here is a gentlemen who wants to see you."

Bella came out. She was dressed very nicely as if she was ready to go for an automobile ride. She looked at me in great surprise.

"I am Morris Shulem," I said introducing myself. "Of course you received the note I mailed you yesterday."

Poor Bella! I thought she would faint. And before I could open my mouth to explain, her mother opened hers:

"The idea! Such an old man! Why, why, you are old enough to be my Bella's grandfather! You misled her into believing that she was corresponding with a man of her age. If you don't leave my house at once I'll get a broomstick!"

"Please, Mrs. Gutkind, don't be angry," I pleaded. "I did not mislead your daughter. I didn't come to get her myself. I am a *shadchen.*"

As soon as the mother heard the word *shadchen* her temper cooled and she began to smile.

So I sat down and told them both how I had bought the pair of socks and how I found the note. "You see," I continued, "the note came to the right party after all."

"But I don't want to get married through a *shadchen*," Bella argued. "It is so old-fashioned. I want to get married in some romantic way. Maybe I'll get another answer, from somebody else. I slipped another note in a pair of socks on the same day I put one in yours. Maybe I'll get some reply yet."

"The chances are that your other note will also fall in the hands of an old man like me," I consoled. "Young men of today don't wear such cheap socks. Why, on my way here, I saw the same socks in a window marked down to ten cents a pair. Please take my advice, Miss Gutkind, and let me find you a fine young man, one that you will really like and be proud of."

Slowly Bella commenced to yield, but she could not forget that she had another note in another pair of socks.

"You need not worry about that," I said reassuringly. "By the time someone finds that other note you will have your name changed, and your address, too."

Two days after, I brought to Bella's house Mr. Barney Kneidel, who was a foreman for a Seventh Avenue manufacturer and earning a good salary.

Mr. Kneidel made a big hit with the whole family, for besides being able to provide well for a wife he was handsome, could sing and was well dressed, too.

"Look at his socks," I whispered to Bella. "You see, they are real silk. What chance was there for him to get your note? He would never have bought those cheap socks."

"You are right, Mr. Shulem," Bella admitted.

They were married in the early fall, a week before Rosh Hashonah. It was, to tell the truth, among the swellest weddings ever celebrated in Brownsville. Pitkin Avenue never looked as gay as on that wedding day of Bella Gut-kind and Barney Kneidel. Both looked extremely happy. Everybody says they never saw such a happy couple in their life.

But after they are married, Mr. Kneidel's salary did not look so big and rather than have Bella cut down, Barney began to economize. The first item to be cut down was silk stockings. "Cotton ones are just as good," he once said to his wife, as he exhibited a new pair of socks that he bought of a pushcart peddler.

One morning when he was getting dressed he unfolded the cheap cotton socks and a slip of paper fell out. He picked it up and read:

> Please write to me.
> BELLA GUTKIND,
> 4444 Pitkin Ave.,
> Brownsville, New York

"*Oy*, Bella, what does this mean?" he demanded.

"Thank heavens!" Bella exclaimed. "My second note, too, fell in the hands of the right man!"

And then Bella told her Barney the whole story. On the same day she telephoned to me of this queer coincidence.

9

A Great Scheme

Once, in the middle of the month of August, I found myself trying to relax in Carol Gonefsky's restaurant. It was in the afternoon, and it felt to me like all of New York was in the restaurant, because after five minutes it was just as hot inside as it was outside. Carol walked over to me and said:

"Morris Shulem, everybody who is anybody is either in the mountains or by the seashore, so what are you doing here?"

What's more, she was right and then and there I thought it would be a good idea to pay a last visit to Arverne, where so many well-to-do families with their grown-up sons and daughters are summering.

I stopped at the Hotel Pinochle, and there I met Mr. Irving Leichter, a young lawyer, a very nice young man. And as I knew that the Gordons are still in Arverne, it struck me that this young lawyer and Mr. Abe Gordon's Janet would make a fine match.

I first called on Mr. Gordon and proposed the *shidduch*. I told him the truth: that at present the lawyer seems to be not much of a success, but with a little influence and encouragement and maybe a little backing, all of which Mr. Gordon could provide, he was sure to make a success.

Mr. Gordon's daughter liked my description of the young man, and now it was up to me to arrange a meeting. That was very easy, for on that evening a dance for the benefit of the Consumptive Aid Society Organization was given at the Hotel Pinochle, where Lawyer Leichter and I were stopping.

"I shall come there with my wife and daughter," Mr. Gordon said, "but please don't tell the young man anything at present, for in case my daughter does not like him I don't want him to feel slighted. Just introduce him without letting him know the purpose."

I did exactly as I was told, and to my great surprise and joy the young man made a good impression on both father and daughter. Later, after the dance was over, when I told Mr. Leichter for what purpose the girl and her father came, he became angry, saying:

"You have been trying to sell me, have you? Well, well, all I can say is that I'll never marry through a *shadchen*. Never! What are you trying to use me for, like a chattel? No, never mind the apologies. It's settled. Good night!"

The young lawyer walked away, and though I did not know this word "chattel," I felt, however, it was a legal expression. I knew I would find Judge Epstein in the card room and asked him to explain this "chattel" to me.

It took ten minutes for the Judge to explain one word to me. He made it sound like he was giving a report to a jury.

It was too late to talk further with Mr. Leichter that evening so I went uneasily to sleep.

At breakfast the next morning I saw Mr. Leichter sitting alone by the window in the coffee shop of the hotel, and I asked the waitress to seat me at his table.

I started our conversation with him by saying:

"Such girls as Janet Gordon are hard to find nowadays. Why don't you think it over."

"I have nothing against Miss Gordon," he replied firmly. "Maybe if I had met her in another way I would have liked her, but this *shadchen* business is not to my taste."

All morning I was thinking of the young man's last words, when he said, "Maybe if I had met her in another way I would have liked her." So what other way could it be?

Arverne was never a lucky place for me. I always met disappointment there. Last summer, when I was in Arverne, I brought together a young businessman with a Queen of Sheba, a $10,000 widow, and the match was nearly settled. But on one nice afternoon, as the widow was bathing in the surf, she got a little too far and was nearly drowned. A young man who was peddling ice-cream bars on the beach jumped in the water and saved her. Out of gratitude the widow married the peddler, and all my work was lost.

As I was sitting on the porch in a rocking chair and thinking, I remembered the widow and the peddler, and a scheme flashed through my mind.

Just before lunch I went to see Mr. Gordon.

"*Nu*, Mr. Shulem?" he asked.

"*Tzoris*," I replied.

"Is it possible that that little shyster did not like my daughter?" Mr. Gordon was more than indignant. "To tell the truth I am surprised my Janet cares for him. I think she fell in love with his manners."

"Mr. Gordon," I tried to explain, "I am sure that he does like your daughter. He is just the kind of a man that a girl like Miss Janet would appeal to, for he is short and thin and your daughter is tall and plump. But he is one of the new kind of philosophers who are opposed to marrying through a *shadchen*. He told me that if he met your daughter in any other way, he would have liked her very much. Now, you see?"

Then I told him of my experience last year with the $10,000 widow who married the rescuer, the ice-cream peddler, and if such a plan could be arranged with his daughter, it would surely work.

"Your daughter," I explained, "would have to appear in a fancy bathing suit about three in the afternoon. That is the time Leichter takes a swim. She must attract his attention of course. After making sure that he noticed her, let her go in the water as far as she can. The rest you can leave to her good sense. He will run in and save her."

"And if not?"

"Such a question! Mr. Gordon!" I was becoming impatient. "He will. He likes her and he will be glad of playing hero, and then it will be the right thing for him to marry her."

All that was needed now was to get Miss Janet's consent, and that was not as easy as we thought. We had to make her to understand that if she really wanted the young lawyer, this was the only way.

At last, she consented.

"Remember," I said as I left them, "he is there about three in the afternoon."

"I shall be there on time," Janet answered, blushing a little bit.

I was at the place an hour before the appointed time. There were not many people on the beach, for that afternoon the skies were cloudy and the weather cool.

Just at three o'clock I saw Janet Gordon strolling on the beach, and all my doubts passed away. Some girls look pretty only in fur coats, but for a girl like Janet, a bathing suit. . . . Enough to make an old *shadchen* young again. And she walked with the air of a queen. And in two or three minutes Lawyer Leichter, also in a bathing suit, comes out from the other side. Miss Gordon recognized him with a smile and he acknowledged with a bow.

Just as Janet got in the water, an ice-cream-bar peddler appeared on the beach. Well, I do not need to tell you that I got scared. Ice-cream peddlers on the beach are bad luck for *shadchens*. But there I saw Mr. Gordon running after the peddler, and as he caught up with him Mr. Gordon asked the peddler if he could supply him with two hundred ice-cream bars for an engagement party next evening.

My ears were listening to the bargaining between Mr. Gordon and the peddler, but my eyes were on the water. I saw Miss Gordon approaching near the lines. My heart beat with joy when I heard a soprano voice cry out: "Save me! Save me! Help! Help!"

"Eighteen dollars is a good price for two hundred ice-cream bars," I heard Mr. Gordon's voice saying at the same time. "I'll give you eighteen fifty."

"Give him eighteen seventy-five!" I yelled to Mr. Gordon, seeing that the peddler turned his face toward the water.

But Mr. Leichter was already in the water and making headway for the spot where Janet Gordon was seen struggling with the waves. The people on the beach cheered. Leichter got hold of her, but—we never thought of that!— he could not lift her, he could not even move her, for he weighed 120 and she 180. All of a sudden he slipped and fell into the water.

Mr. Gordon and I stood with bated breath. For a moment both disappeared under the water. Then we saw Janet Gordon coming out, carrying Lawyer Leichter fondly in her arms. The cheering crowd was now giggling and laughing at the strange turn of the heroic act.

The same afternoon Lawyer Leichter left Arverne.

The next evening, as I was sitting with Mr. Gordon on the porch, talking over the sad miscalculation, the ice-cream peddler with a heavy basket appeared, and stepping up to Mr. Gordon, he announced:

"I have brought you the two hundred ice-cream bars. I'll let you have them for eighteen seventy-five, as you said."

Mr. Gordon nearly fainted.

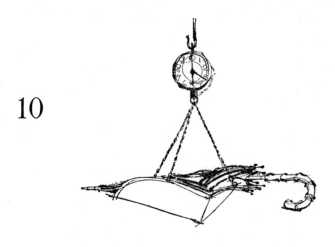

10

And the Shadchen Still Pursued Him

"Hello, **Mr.** Shulem," Joe greeted me with a worried look as I walked into Carol Gonefsky's Café and Restaurant. "Please sit down, I'll bring you something with tea, yes? And have I a story to tell you?"

What could I do but listen?

"Bercovich the *shadchen* was here again last Wednesday, and it was he who got me into a new mess. 'Listen, Mr. Bercovich,' I said before he could open his mouth, 'it is no use, I don't want to listen to your proposals. I don't intend to get married. I don't want to get married—and that's that!'

" 'But how about going to another man's wedding?' he asked me. 'Just for fun,' he added. 'Going to another man's wedding you assume no more risk than going to another man's funeral.'

" 'Whose wedding is it, anyhow?' I asked.

" 'Oh, you don't know him yet,' the *shadchen* answered, 'but you'll get an invitation and you'll become acquainted. You must promise me to come.'

"I was puzzled. I could not understand how and why I was going to be invited to a wedding of people I never heard of. But after Bercovich explained, everything looked very simple. Maybe you already have heard that there are special stores in the city where you can hire wedding clothes and wedding presents, and offices where you can get people to act as your uncles, aunts or cousins, if you have no relations of your own in this country. You see, people like swell weddings, with a big band, lots of wedding presents and a whole lot of *mishpocho*—all kinds of relatives and plenty of them. Now, as Bercovich explained to me, he wanted me to act as uncle for the bridegroom, who was his client.

" 'There will be no trouble for you at all,' Bercovich said. 'The wedding takes place next Sunday night. In the afternoon I will bring you an alarm clock, which you will take along as your wedding present. The groom has already paid the twenty-five cents rental for the clock, and all you do is to eat, drink, be merry, and let the groom call you uncle.'

" 'I'll go,' I said, 'but I hope that there will be no trouble.'

" 'Oh, there will be no trouble at all,' he assured me.

"Friday I received an invitation to the wedding and Sunday afternoon Bercovich brought me the alarm clock which I was to bring as a wedding present to my new nephew. In the evening I put on my tuxedo and went to attend the wedding of Sol Greenspon and Jenny Segal, which was to take place at the Zion Hall that night.

"Coming to the place, I check my hat and then I go

right through the open door, on the ground floor, where I see lots of people dressed in style and looking jolly.

" 'I am the uncle of the bridegroom,' I introduced myself to a man who seemed to be one of the nearest kin.

" 'I am very pleased to meet you,' he said.

" 'I am the bride's father. Come and meet my daughter. She'll be delighted.'

"Taking me under my arm, he led me to the bride, who was sitting with her bridesmaids and the women of her family in a little room at the other end of the large dance hall, where she was waiting for the groom to come and lead to the *chupah*.

" 'This is the *choson*'s uncle,' the bride's father introduced me.

"The bride stood up. She looked so lovely in her bridal gown that I would not mind marrying her myself. Then she threw her veil aside and gave me a kiss on each cheek. My heart nearly melted away and I was so confused that I clumsily kissed her on her little pug nose.

" 'And this is his present,' the bride's father said, taking the alarm clock from me. Those kisses made me so dizzy that I forgot about the wedding present which I had brought with me.

" 'Thank you, Uncle,' the bride said. 'This is a very beautiful clock. I shall give it a place of honor on our mantelpiece, and every morning when it rings I will surely think of you.'

"Then the *choson* himself came in. He looked at me, looked me up and down from my hat to my shoes.

" 'Why, don't you know your uncle?' the bride asked him. 'Look at the lovely present he brought us,' and she showed him the alarm clock, which was put on a table with other presents for exhibition.

" 'I think the gentleman made a mistake,' the *choson*

said. 'I have enough uncles of my own and they are all here, plenty of them, in the next room.'

"Then, turning to me, the *choson* said:

"'There is another wedding going on upstairs. Maybe that is where your nephew is getting married.'

"I ran for the door, forgetting about the alarm clock. I went upstairs. Sure, here was another wedding going on. Bercovich met me at the door.

"'You are a little late,' he said to me; 'they are all waiting for you. But you forgot to bring the wedding present.'

"'The wedding present is here,' I said, 'but I delivered it to the wrong party.' Then I told him the rest.

"To save me from humiliation, Bercovich went down himself to demand the alarm clock, and in a few minutes he came back with it, and he led me into the hall.

"Here I was introduced to the other bride. I received some kisses, but they did not taste as sweet as those I had downstairs. For this bride who was to marry my 'nephew' was a widow and the mother of four children.

"The bridegroom was glad to see me, of course, and he introduced me to everybody and to the bride's two uncles. I thought her uncles were the real stuff, but I soon found out they were not.

"After the wedding supper, as I was standing and watching the young people dance, I noticed the two uncles of the bride having a serious conversation between themselves, and from the way they looked at me I understood that I was the subject of their talk. I don't know why, but I began to feel nervous and sincerely wished that the wedding was over.

"At last the bride's two uncles came over to me and one of them asked:

"'Are you a real uncle or a hired one?'

"Here Bercovich came to my rescue. I suppose he saw trouble coming, so he came up in time to save me.

" 'What funny questions you ask!' Bercovich laughed at him. 'Sure he is a real uncle. His mother, *oleho hasholem*, and the *choson*'s mother, *oleho hasholem*, were twin sisters.'

" 'Now, you see,' one of the bride's uncles said, pointing his finger right in the *shadchen*'s face, 'the *choson* told us a different story—that the man's father and his father were twin brothers. It is a fake; anyone can see that.'

" 'Well,' argued Bercovich, 'couldn't the twin brothers marry the twin sisters?'

" 'Mister Bercovich,' the other of the two uncles butted in, 'don't you try such bluffs on us; we are not from Brownsville.' And then, turning to me, he said:

" 'You see, young man, we are members of the Amalgamated Uncles, Aunts, and Cousins Protective Association. We are a strong organization, and unless you are a bona fide member of the union you can't be an uncle. You will have to pay the usual $10 fine, or we shall make charges against you at the next meeting of the Waiters' Union. Ten dollars is a small fine in comparison with your offense against organized labor. You may go home now. Our walking delegate will call on you and collect the fine!'

"I left the hall as fast as my legs could carry me. And now I am asking you, does it pay to be good? It cost me $10 just because that Bercovich wanted me to do a favor. Never again!"

"I'll have another glass of tea, Joe, please," I said, feeling sorry for the unhappy waiter.

11

The Bachelor's Ideal

I was to a wedding about three months ago, and there I noticed a fine young man, far away in his thirties—maybe at the end of them—who seemed to be very much popular with the ladies. He joked with them, he *kibitzed* them, and it seemed to me that they liked him, too.

"A fine young man like you," I said to him, "ought to have a girl of his own and be happy with her."

"Oh, I know you, you are Mr. Shulem the *shadchen,*" he greeted me. "How do you do?"

"Thank you," I said. "I am happy, for I have a wife and children and a home. Can you say the same of yourself?"

He gave me a look, and such a look I had seen before. "Tell me more," it said.

"No, you tell me," I said to him. "What do you want? Is it money, or a fine girl, or both?"

"No, money is not my object," he answered, "I'm looking for an ideal."

"And what's your ideal?"

"In the first place," he said, "she must be a girl of education, and of good background. She must also be beautiful. My idea of beauty is a tall, graceful girl. Well shaped with dark hair and black eyes. If you find me a girl like that I'll marry her, even if she has not a penny to her name."

"I have such a girl," I said. "She is just exactly in every particular as you pictured her, only she is not tall. She is maybe the height like the bride."

"That sounds interesting to me," the gentleman said, "and let me introduce myself, my name is Gulash, Tzadik Gulash. Remember, Mr. Shulem, I am not an impressionable boy. I'm climbing in years and in these years I've made a very good dollar and an even better study of the female species."

Well Shulem, I said to myself, *oy, oy, oy,* take care, you're in for another ride with special instructions. "Mr. Gulash," I said finally after catching my breath from the shock of my new friend's study of the female species, "what have you learned from your studies?"

"First of all, the studies explain the pitfalls marriage has in store for the human race," Mr. Gulash started to explain. "What changes take place as the silver begins to streak in our hair."

I am already beside myself when I start listening to this kind of *meshugaas* and I was looking for a way to say, "I beg your pardon, but I see somebody I must talk to." But before I could pull my wits together Tzadik called to his cousin, who was also popular with the ladies.

The cousin came over and Tzadik said, "Mr. Shulem please shake hands with my cousin on my mother's side, Mr. Edward Clay Rabinowitz."

What could I do but say, "How do you do?" and shook hands.

"Edward," continued Gulash, "Mr. Shulem's a *shadchen*, and he wants to know why I'm not married. For the same reason you are not married. It is like this, Mr. Shadchen, Edward and I have made a real study of the human race, specializing in the female."

"What's this specialty?" I wanted to know.

"Well," Mr. Rabinowitz started, "a couple of years ago I was in love with Molly, the bride. Her father wanted to put me up in any business I wanted and—"

"He is the weaker one of us two," interrupted Mr. Gulash.

"Go on Mr. Rabinowitz." I wanted to know more. "And who was your *shadchen?*"

"There was no marriage broker involved, Mr. Shulem," Mr. Rabinowitz said.

"So that's why you two parties fell apart," I said. "A good *shadchen* knows how to keep a deal active and to a conclusion."

"No, that is not it at all," said Rabinowitz. "My cousin Tzadik began to interest me in the female species."

"What kind of talk is that, it is a shame to speak with such a free tongue about the nice things in life," I said. "A home, a family, good meals, a clean shirt. What has species got to do?"

"You don't understand, I must explain," continued Rabinowitz. "Tzadik proved to me by the Darwin theory that physical traits are hereditary. By viewing a girl and then her mother you have a clear picture of what the girl will look like in twenty years from now."

"It doesn't make sense," I said, and I was ready to walk away.

"Thin girls have thin mothers," said Gulash, "fat girls with eyeglasses have fat mothers with eyeglasses."

"And the father has nothing to do with it?" I wanted to know.

"Up to this point our study is with the female," said Gulash. "It should take not too many *bar mitzvahs*, engagement parties and weddings to complete the study."

"I think you are just free *fressers* when you limit your study to happy occasions," I said.

"Oh, no," both of them said at one time.

"It is at such affairs," continued Rabinowitz, "we have the chance to see the mother and daughter, and sometimes even a third generation like here; Molly's grandmother is here."

"To me this is nonsense," I said. "You, Mr. Rabinowitz, for breaking the engagement to Molly, almost gave her a setback. For a long time she would not go out, even to a picture, and I had to spend many hours in telling her what a good-for-nothing, without even knowing you, you surely must have been. Look, Molly's mother is maybe a size forty-four and Molly is a . . . maybe size thirty-six and the *bubbie* is shrunk down to a maybe thirty-two. What's this species? Life is a gamble, so make the best of it and exercise. Here's my card and if you get out of your foolishness I'll introduce you. Good-by and have a good time."

Maybe two days later each man called me separately and gave me descriptions of what they were looking for—but it should be without a *shadchen*. They don't believe in a *shadchen*, but a fee they'll gladly pay personally.

I figure the best thing for me to do with the cousins was to find for them orphans. So they couldn't bother with species.

"Minnie," I called to my wife after the second telephone.

"Give me an advice. Who is a girl have I got in mind who has no family here?"

"How about our daughter-in-law's second cousin from Philadelphia," said Minnie. "Morris, she is staying with our son Alvin on her 'sabical'!"

"Oh, the schoolteacher," I answered. "And you mean sabbatical. You know what a sabbatical is?"

"No, so what is a sabical?"

"A schoolteacher gets a year's vacation with pay, besides the summer vacation," I informed my wife, "after every seven years' teaching."

"So she can spend a year looking for a husband," said Minnie.

"Yes, and I think Charlotte will be good for that Gulash," I said. "A teacher she is and maybe she can teach him. Family she has not, so his species business is *kapoot*."

I telephoned my son Alvin and asked if Charlotte was available because I think I can make a match.

"Available," Alvin shouted, "Why, Papa, she'll travel!"

I don't always understand my own children, so you can understand how I can get mixed up with strangers.

I called up Tzadik Gulash and made an arrangement for him to meet Charlotte, the schoolteacher without a family from Philly, for the next night. He came by my house and then we walked the six blocks to Alvin's.

"How old is she?" Tzadik asked me while walking.

"I don't know, old she is not," I answered. "I haven't seen her in a few years now. She lives in Philadelphia."

Well, when we walked into Alvin's house I thought poor Tzadik would pass out. His ideal was to be tall and graceful with dark hair and eyes. I haven't seen the girl since my son's wedding, which was sixteen years ago, and Charlotte was then a girl of fifteen.

Only one look did I give at her, and my blood froze in my veins. Not that she was so homely. I marry off much homelier girls, with no work at all. But that cousin of my daughter-in-law's was just the opposite of Mr. Gulash's ideal. The Philadelphia girl was medium height, stubby, brown eyes and with red hair.

At first Mr. Gulash lost his speech, but the girl, I could see, was clever and talkative, and she soon dragged him into conversation. Five minutes later my son made signs to me to come out with him, and we left the pair *shmoosing* as if they were old acquaintances.

I went home. Next day Mr. Gulash came to me and he was almost crying.

"Please, Mr. Shulem," he begged me, "get me out of it. I was foolish enough to promise Miss Charlotte to call again. Please, Mr. Shulem," he continued pleading, "how much will you charge me to buy back the introduction!"

"Forget it," I said. "You don't have to buy nothing or keep that promise. Maybe you have been imposed upon."

He was glad of my advice, and went away.

About two weeks later I met both men, Edward Clay Rabinowitz and his cousin Tzadik Gulash, at Gonefsky's and the men were in a heated argument. I was sorry I came in to the café, and before I could turn around they both greeted me.

"Gentlemen, how do you do!" I said with a forced smile. "And how is the world treating the female species investigators?"

"Please, Mr. Shulem," Gulash beseeched, "give us an advice on what to do. As a gentleman I kept my promise to call on Miss Charlotte again, and on every call I give a new promise. It is true, she is a fine girl, but not my ideal of beauty."

"So what do you want from me?" I asked.

"Well, after about three calls," said Gulash, "I took my cousin along for support to get me out of my next promise to call again. But what do you think happened? He liked her and now I like her too!"

"But what about your species study?" I couldn't resist but ask.

"Oh, I will try to forget all about it," said Rabinowitz. "I'll take the girl as is. I have already prepared my family tree."

"What kind of a tree?" I asked.

"Charlotte wants for us to present to her in writing our family history," said Rabinowitz, "so she can study our blood lines and how sturdy our stock is."

"I already bought Charlotte an engagement ring," chimed in Gulash.

"Boys, wait a minute," I said. "Since I'm responsible for the introduction, I am responsible for the results. Meet me here at eleven o'clock tonight and I'll try and straighten everything out."

It was agreed, and I left for Alvin's house. When I arrived there Charlotte was packing her satchel and was in a gay happy mood.

"Where are you going, Charlotte, and in such a hurry?" I asked.

"Mr. Shulem," Charlotte answered, "since I met Tzadik and Edward Clay, I have been dizzy. First with their theories and second with their ideas and ideals. Today in the library, I met the history teacher from my school in Philadelphia, he's on a sabbatical leave also, and we compared our family trees and found we are suited for one another. So tonight at eight o'clock we are eloping. Do you want to come along and watch us elope?"

"*Mazel tov,*" I said. "No thank you, I've got a pair of cousins to see in a couple of hours."

By night I walked to the restaurant and was greeted by Joe Katzman, the waiter, with, "Benchy and his ma and pa just left and they told the two men you saw here this afternoon about an elopement and the men started to holler on one another with 'You and your ideas' and the other answered, 'You had no right to butt in.' Finally your son Alvin talked to them and quieted them down. Two minutes ago they left and asked me to give you this note."

> We are making a partnership and will become marriage counselors.
>
> Gulash and Rabinowitz

Now I ask you, does it pay to be a good fellow?

12

My Enemies Should Have Business with Women

Was it Mr. Keats or Mr. Shelley Berman the philosopher who once said, "It is better to have loved and lost than never to have loved at all"? Except for James Henry Shapiro. Because no matter what happens, all he can do is lose.

Why do some people stop a doctor on the street and ask his opinion of a symptom which is being attended to by another physician? I assure you, no doctor likes it. So when Mrs. Greenberg came to me to ask for an advice of Mr. James Henry Shapiro, the young man who was keeping company with her daughter, I was annoyed. That is one of the nuisances a *shadchen* meets in life.

"Why do you ask me, Mrs. Greenberg?" I said, "let it be

with *mazel*. She got the poor fellow on the string, so there is nothing left for me but to wish you and your daughter good luck."

"Thank you," she replied. "I know you wish it to us from the bottom of your heart. And you know, Mr. Shulem, he is such a fine young man, and he has a government position; he is a letter carrier."

"I think I heard that he is a driver for a smoked-fish concern," I remarked.

"What!" the woman yelled at me. "Is that a fact?"

The same day Mrs. Greenberg put the question straight to her daughter's intended, and he confessed to her that he was not a letter carrier, not even a full-fledged driver, but an assistant to the driver, who delivers all kinds of smoked and pickled fish for Brodsky & Chambers.

On the same day Mrs. Greenberg's daughter Rosalie broke her engagement and told her would-be *choson* not to show his face again in her presence.

It was hoped that the incident would be finished then and there, but the next day Mrs. Greenberg dropped in my house and she was almost out of breath when she cried out:

"Mr. Shulem, save him, please save him. Save all of us!"

"Save who? What happened?" I asked.

"My Rosalie got a letter from him this morning saying that he can't live without her, he is going to do away with himself, and that by the time she will read his letter he'll be dead."

I rushed out and bought every morning newspaper that was on the corner newsstand; I even sent for Benchy, my grandson, and asked him to help me look for items of suicide.

There was none on that day, but maybe, I thought, Shapiro died after the newspapers were already out. So I told Mrs. Greenberg to wait for the afternoon papers. In

78

the meantime I telephoned his employers, asking them if they had any information of their assistant driver.

"He took a three-day vacation," was the answer over the telephone.

"He fooled you," I said. "It was just an idea to get away and commit suicide."

"Suicide!" the voice over the telephone repeated. "Why, that Shapiro just telephoned us an order on his way to Rockaway Beach, where he is going to spend his vacation."

That was enough for me. So I hung up the receiver and began to think hard of what I was to do, for now I was almost sure that the fellow made a bluff.

About two in the same afternoon, Mrs. Greenberg came again, her eyes red from crying.

"*Oy*, Mr. Shulem," she said, "I don't think my daughter will be able to stand it. She will die of remorse. She is crying like a baby and is heartbroken over the poor fellow. If it was only possible that he may return alive!"

"Would she marry him then?" I asked.

"Such a question!" the woman answered. "And I assure you my Rosalie would love him ten times as much as she loved him before. But what is the use? He is surely dead now, and not even the papers know what became of him."

After a moment's silence, she added:

"Mr. Shulem, maybe has come a miracle and he is still living. Maybe the water was too shallow, or the revolver was empty, or the poison failed to work, or he was caught by a clothesline when he jumped from the roof."

"Well," I said, "let us hope and wait. Maybe he is in some hospital with a broken leg, or otherwise crippled. So what would be the use for your girl to marry such a man, when I can get her the handsomest young man in New York?"

"Oh, no, don't say that," the woman protested. "If he is

only alive, my daughter would marry him no matter what physical condition he is."

"She will change her mind," I said, "when she will see the fellow I am thinking about for her. Just watch. I'll come to you this evening."

I took my brief case and umbrella and went straight to Rockaway Beach. It was just the day for bathing, and I walked along the beach, looking at every young man, whether he had curly dark hair and a curled-up mustache like Shapiro's, whom I had seen only once before.

After walking two hours I found Shapiro lying asleep on the sand in the shade of a wooden fence. He was snoring.

I got a hold of him and, giving him a good shake, I said:

"Why do you lie on the ground? You ought to be under the ground."

He opened his eyes and stared at me.

"You are a fine fellow!" I said. "Enjoying yourself here, while Rosalie is mourning and is crying her eyes out for you."

"Rosalie? How do you know?" he asked. "Who are you?"

"I am Shulem the *shadchen*," I said. "Here to take you back to Rosalie. You scared the life out of that poor girl, but she loves you now ten times as much as she ever loved you before. You are a good-for-nothing, but she'll marry you, just the same. Come. I'll take you to her."

He got up, shook the sand off his linen suit, and we started toward the station.

In an hour we reached the house where lived Rosalie and her mother. I had the young man stay outside the house, and I went in to prepare the women for the surprise. I broke the news gently. First, I told them that I found him with both legs broken; then I said that he broke only one, and at last I told them that he was merely sunburned. The ladies were overjoyed.

But when I brought him in, there was a sudden change in Rosalie's manner. She came up to Shapiro, looked straight in his eyes and then said:

"Go 'way, you coward! I don't want you!"

My enemies should have business with women and philosophers, Mr. Keats or Mr. Berman.

13

Celia and the Poet

Some people are embarrassed to discuss their marital problems with a marriage broker. After all, when you have a toothache, you go to a dentist. He's got the education and the experience to relieve the pain and correct the ache. The same goes with a *shadchen*. Over the years a successful *shadchen* sees and handles all sorts of arrangements of the heart. And there are cases like dentists have, clinical cases, where the *shadchen* does not receive a fee. It is these kind of clinical cases that give him additional experience in making successful long-lasting matches.

Leah Lifshitz was in her youth a very pretty girl. Her father was one of the wealthier men in his town. But Leah married for love and against the advice of her father. Her husband was a poor man, whom she met at a cousin's *bar mitzvah*. Him—her husband—she lost after bringing into the world four little girls.

Many times I advised Mrs. Lifshitz to marry again, but she refused my advice.

"No, Mr. Shulem," she would say, "not the best man in this world would I marry. I don't want to give my children a step-father. Maybe someday you will *shadchen* my girls."

Whenever I would meet Mrs. Lifshitz she always had some news about her girls. She worked as a practical nurse, and managed to feed and clothe her four and to give them an education. One day I met her—it was about two years ago—she told me:

"Oh, Mr. Shulem, you don't know how happy I am to-day. Believe me, you are the only friend that is really interested in my poor little orphans, *nebich*. My youngest, Fanny, already she's got a job. Now all my children are working and earning enough for a living, so I don't have to work so hard any more."

It was good news to hear. I knew that Celia and Freda were working in a department store, Jenny was a typist, and now the youngest was doing general work in a large mail-order house.

"Pretty soon," I said to Mrs. Lifshitz, "I'll have to look for some nice gentlemen for your daughters."

"Pretty soon, yes," she answered, "but my girls have no money and there is hardly a chance that they will have much of it later. You have no idea, Mr. Shulem, what it costs a girl nowadays to be well dressed."

"Don't worry," I consoled, "just encourage your daughters to look pretty. You remember the proverb, 'A pretty face is half a *nadan*.'"

A few weeks later I met her again.

"And how are the girls?" I inquire.

"My darlings, they are just fine," the mother replies. "Only it is hard for them to save money, even hard to save

for a new hat. Listen to what I'll tell you and you will be
surprised. My daughters needed new hats, but they could
not spend more than four dollars for a hat each. That was
all their budget would allow. Then my oldest girl, Celia,
said, 'Why should we buy four cheap hats at four dollars
each? Let us buy one good hat for fifteen or sixteen dollars
and we'll wear it in turns.' The other girls like the idea
and agree; now they have a hat that is like Park Avenue.
Did you ever see sisters live so friendly and so devoted?"

"You ought to be proud of them, Mrs. Lifshitz," I said
to her. "Such sensible girls."

The next time we met she told me a similar story. Her
daughters were about to get new dresses at around twelve
to fourteen dollars for each dress. But after discussing it
between themselves, the girls decide the old dresses are
maybe good enough for everyday wear, and only for special
occasions would they get one fine dress for fifty or sixty
dollars.

"Very sensible," I complimented. "Your girls have practical minds."

After that I did not see the woman for quite some while,
but once in the summer, on a hot Sunday, my Minnie and
I went to Coney Island to get a breath of sea air. There, at
the beach, I met Mrs. Lifshitz and three of her daughters.

"And Celia?" I asked, seeing that the eldest sister was
missing.

"She is on her vacation in Tannersville." Mrs. Lifshitz
smiled at me. "Only one of my girls is having a vacation
this year."

"Why can't the other girls, too, have a vacation?" I
asked.

"My girls talked it over and decided that, like their hats
and dresses, instead of all of them taking just a so-so vacation, the oldest sister will go to a fancy resort. Mr. Shulem,

what chance is there for a girl to meet a fine young man in a cheap summer resort? All a girl can meet in these places are nothings and *schnorrers*. So my three youngest gave their vacation money to Celia and she went to Tannersville for two weeks."

I felt a little uneasy when I heard that Celia was trying to find a husband for herself without me. But then who could blame the poor girl? She knew that she could not get much of a party in the regular way, so she was speculating on a chance that some wealthy young man would fall in love with her and overlook that fact that she is a poor girl.

"I wish her luck, and should your Celia need my help, believe me, I am ready to do anything for her," I tell Mrs. Lifshitz.

The woman thanks me and I go my way. Ten days later she is at my house with a tale of woe.

"My Celia is back," she said to me, looking very sad.

"Well, of course, she had to come back," I answered. "Did you expect her to stay there all summer?"

"I meant to say," she explained, "that Celia came back very disappointed. She met a young man in Tannersville who looked like a millionaire or a millionaire's son. They liked each other as soon as they met. He came there Friday. Sunday he told Celia his secret. He is a lawyer's clerk and that instead of going to a cheap resort for two weeks he thought it wiser to spend his vacation allowance on one good weekend in an expensive place where he can meet fashionable people. Now, can you imagine how my daughter felt when she heard that?"

"Well," I said, placing my hands on my stomach, "it is an old game played every year at the summer resorts. Tell Celia not to worry. Celia will get a husband, and a good one, too."

But the woman was inconsolable. "So much money

thrown away, and my other girls deprived of their vacation."

So the summer passed and vacationers began to flock
back to the city. My fall business prospects looked good
and I expected to be busy finishing up matches that started
in summer resorts. One day as I was planning to go out
for business, Mrs. Lifshitz, whom I had not seen for weeks,
dropped in.

"I'll be but a minute," she said, seeing my brief case and
umbrella in my hand. "I came to you about this. Maybe
you could find a young man for Celia? She has eight hundred dollars now."

"Eight hundred dollars?" I asked. "Where did she get
it?"

"My girls had two hundred each saved in the bank,"
Mrs. Lifshitz confided. "But there is little chance to get
a real nice young man with only two hundred dollars
nadan. They decided to give all their money to Celia, so
that she may get something real nice."

"I'll try my best," I said, though in my heart I doubted
that I could do anything for the girl. What is eight hundred dollars nowadays?

Again some weeks pass. One day, when I return home
from an engagement party, Minnie breaks the news that
Celia Lifshitz got a nice young man, handsome, educated—
a perfect gentleman. Celia met him at an affair of the Boi-
briker *Landsleite* Society.

"And you could not get her a husband!" my wife
mocked.

"The Lord helps those who help themselves," I replied.
"I only hope she got the right man."

It was a short engagement and a speedy wedding. Two
months after Celia was married I met her mother.

"How is the *kalle* getting along?" I inquired.

"Oh, she is getting along splendidly," Mrs. Lifshitz said. "And all of us are happy on account of that. But—"

"But what?"

"He can't make a living. He is too educated to work in a shop or factory, and he is too honest to go in business. So he sits home all day and reads and writes poetry."

"So he is a poet! Maybe he can make money out of his poetry," I suggested.

"The trouble is that he can't make money even of his poetry," Mrs. Lifshitz explained. "He says that editors are too ignorant to understand his poetry. All the editors want, my son-in-law says, is nonsense in rhymes, but he writes deep, without rhymes. He calls it blanket verse."

"You mean blank verse," I corrected. "I have heard of such a thing."

"Celia wanted to go back to work," Mrs. Lifshitz continued. "But my other girls, God bless them, won't let her. They support her and Alfred. They supply him with plenty of pin money, for he likes to go to the literary coffeehouses, and he smokes imported cigarettes, and is fond of fancy neckties. Oh, Mr. Shulem, you should hear him read poetry! I may not get the meaning, but I can feel it. He is a wonderful young man, a genius. And we are all so happy!"

And as she turned away to leave I heard her sigh.

Like I have said before many times—when you have a toothache, you go to a good dentist. And I wouldn't have charged Celia one cent for a fee!

14

The Tannersville Villa

One of the love-at-first-sight matches in which I was the *shadchen* happened about two years ago. Simon Malbin, the shirt manufacturer, married Frances Shenker. He was an elderly confirmed bachelor and she was a talented and pretty girl. As soon as I introduced them, they fell in love with each other and to such an extent that it was perfectly safe for me to leave them to themselves until their wedding day, when I got my check.

"Mr. Shulem, I beg of you. Remain our friend," Malbin said when he handed me my check. "The amount of this check is but a trifle in comparison to the happiness you have brought me by finding for me such a darling as Frances. Please, you and your wife pay us a visit to our villa in Tannersville."

It warms a *shadchen*'s heart to see how contented two people in love can be.

During that summer I was thinking of the invitation often, but every time I mention it my wife said "not yet," saying it would be better to leave the newlyweds alone and not to intrude upon them during their first summer of wedded bliss.

But the next summer, which was a year ago, I happened to meet Simon Malbin on a ferryboat and he reminded me of my promise to visit him in his "Garden of Eden."

"This summer we shall go," said Minnie when I told her of meeting Mr. Malbin.

Minnie and I planned. The Fourth of July weekend we deliberately omitted and the same for the Labor Day weekend. We settled on the third weekend in July.

When we arrived we found the villa crowded with people, young and old, men and women. "Maybe your Mr. Malbin is conducting a boardinghouse and he is going to charge us for our board," Minnie suspected. But I could hardly believe it, and Minnie's suspicions were proved wrong on the same day.

In the evening Malbin took us out for a walk and confidentially he explained who his guests were.

"It was all right for Adam and Eve to enjoy life in the Garden of Eden," he said, "because they had no uncles, or aunts, or cousins, or second cousins to invite themselves to their place and to make their existence miserable. But Frances and I have so many relations and their number increasing constantly, that we sometimes think of selling the place to get rid of them. Mr. Shulem, maybe you should know of a party who would like to buy a summer home?"

"I'm only a *shadchen*," I said, "and not in the real estate business. But, tell me, how did it all begin?"

"It began last year about this time," Mr. Malbin related. "Just a week after we had settled here, an old lady accompanied by a young man came here. The young man, who was the old lady's son-in-law, announced that the old lady was my wife's mother's second cousin, and she was convalescing. He thought this place of ours was just the place for her to convalesce. He also said he could not trust the care of his dear mother-in-law to anybody else but to me and my wife. So he left her here and the woman stayed with us six weeks.

"A few days after, came a party of four. The leader was a young man who introduced himself as my cousin. He was engaged to a young girl who was in the party, and as he was very anxious to see me and to spend a few days with me, and as his future mother-in-law did not think it proper for her daughter to go out of town unchaperoned, he took along the mother, too. Of course, the youngest child, a litle girl of seven, who could not be left without her mother, had to be included in the party."

And this was only the beginning of Malbin's troubles. The young man, who came with his intended, her mother and her little sister, had a camera with him, and he took snapshots of the house and the surroundings and sent out the prints to all of his relations and to the relations of his intended. After that, they began to arrive in big bunches and they kept coming the following summer.

As we walked back to the house I noticed a middle-aged woman carry two suitcases from the house and deposit them on the porch.

"*Mazel tov!*" I said to Malbin, "one of your aunts is leaving."

But I made a wrong guess, for as soon as Mrs. Malbin saw the woman on the porch she nearly fainted. "Why, that's our cook!" she cried, and ran toward the porch.

"When you engaged me," I heard the cook say, "you told me that you were only a young, childless couple, and now I have to cook for fifteen. I thought that would be the most, but today you got two more,"—pointing at me and my wife. "For heaven's sake! Where do you get so many relations? I am going back to Brooklyn."

Malbin walked over to the cook and whispered something in her ear. It worked like magic. In a second her anger left her and she was all smiles. She begged me and my wife to forgive her, which we did.

As the cook went back to the kitchen, Mrs. Malbin asked her husband:

"How much did you raise her?"

"Not one penny," he said.

"Then what was the magic word that performed the wonderful miracle?" Mrs. Malbin wanted to know.

"I told her that Mr. Shulem is a *shadchen,* and the old maid changed her mind," the husband explained.

We stayed with the Malbins two weeks and we had a splendid time, and I went home with Minnie, promising to come out again next summer.

Last week I had to go to Tannersville on business, so, after seeing my party, I thought of paying a quick surprise visit to the "Garden of Eden," and to see whether the Malbins still have their uncles, aunts and cousins.

As I came there a servant met me at the door and took my brief case and umbrella. It was a new girl whom I did not see last year, and she informed me that the "missus" and the boss and all the guests went to the village, but they will be back in time for dinner.

"Poor fellow!" I said to myself, "he still has them."

I felt sleepy, so I lay down in the room which the girl had shown me. A rap on the door woke me up. A young man whom I had never seen before came in and, bowing politely, he greeted me with:

"How do you do? May I ask you if you are an uncle or a cousin, and are you related to me or to my wife?"

I stared at him for fully a minute and was greatly confused by his questions. Finally I regained my speech and blurted out:

"I came to visit Mr. Malbin."

"Mr. Malbin is not here any more," the young man answered, and began to smile. "He sold the place to me. I got a real buy, but now I know why he wanted to get rid of it at so low a price."

"Do you get many relations?" I asked.

At this moment a young woman came to the door and inquired of my host:

"Dear, is this gentleman your relation or mine?"

"I'm no relation at all," ventured I in my own behalf. "I came here by mistake, thinking the Malbins still lived here, and now I'm going home." And as I said this I picked up my brief case and here I am.

15

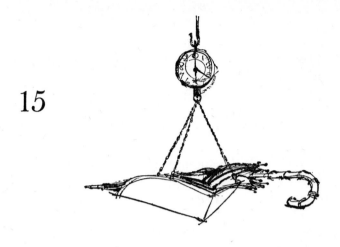

The Real Estater

When Mr. Livingstone finally met Mr. Stanley in Africa, the actual words Mr. Livingstone said to his friend were not "How do you do?" or some such greeting, but "A leopard does not change its spots!" The same with a *shadchen;* once a *shadchen* always a *shadchen.*

Occasionally on a Sunday afternoon, Ziemring, the humorist, would stop by Gonefsky's Restaurant to hear a story and tell a story. It is these Sunday-afternoon tea drinkers that added the word "Kibitzarnie" on to the Gonefsky Restaurant. Carol knew when these *kibitzers* would come in that I wanted to hear their stories and so did Joe Katzman, the waiter. For me it helped to have a new story ready when I would be introducing a party to a party—just in case a laugh was needed. For Joe it was like bread and butter. If a couple comes and sits at his table and they are mad because of slow service, or the husband had a fight with his wife over the mother-in-law, a fresh new story breaks the ice, there are laughs, and Joe makes himself a nice extra tip.

So a couple times a month on Sunday afternoon we ran to Gonefsky's.

I walked in just as Ziemring was telling about a prospective bridegroom who was telling his bride-to-be about his gold mine right in New York City. The bride-to-be laughed and said she had lived here all of her life and if there was even an oil well in New York City she surely would have seen it. The groom became very annoyed and invited his intended and her family to come and see his gold mine. When they arrived at the address the bride shrieked, "Why it's only a junk yard," to which the groom answered, "It may be a junk yard to you, but it nets me $50,000 a year, so it's my gold mine."

This particular Sunday, Golubchik, the comedian from the Second Avenue Theatre, was present. Stories ran back and forth and it seemed like somebody blew a bugle because before long around the table people were standing. I don't know how many deep.

And sure enough who should, as he put it, "drop in" but Bercovich the *shadchen*. The nerve of that man to come to the restaurant where Joe worked after Joe's experience with him.

He worked his way up front and tried to butt in with a story, but he was told to be quiet. Finally he said, "Shulem, I am no longer a *shadchen*, I am now in the real estate business."

Joe Katzman did not believe him and he looked at the clock and saw that it was already time for him to go, even though on Sunday is his afternoon off. But as I leave the restaurant with Joe we notice that Bercovich is following us.

"I am no more a *shadchen*. I gave it up," he said to Joe. "I am a real estater now, and doing fine."

"Is that so?" Joe said, and asked him to tell something about his business.

"To begin with," Bercovich said, "real estate is a very old business. The whole island of Manhattan was once bought from the Indians for $24. Had I been there I would give them $30. Anyhow, the real estaters who bought it were like greenhorns in the business, because they might have gotten it for $14 had they bargained a little longer."

"Are there any more Indians around New York?" I asked.

"Plenty of them," Bercovich said. "Near Flatbush there was some vacant land where an old farmer lived in a hut with lots of ground surrounded by trees; on it there was also a brook with little fishes. A real estater saw the little farm and thought maybe it was worth while buying. He made the old farmer an offer which almost stunned him. Yet it took the farmer a long time to make up his mind to sell the little place where he was born and where his children and grandchildren were born, and where they played baseball and tennis and caught little fishes in the brook. But at last, when the real estater added two or three hundred dollars to his first offer, the old farmer gave in and moved to the city, where he found out that with the money that he had now he could sell vegetables peacefully.

"The real estater cut up the little farm in small lots twenty-five by a hundred and started to build several rows of model two-family houses, to be sold to home seekers. But when the houses were about ready to be sold or rented some multimillionaire passed by and took a fancy to the spot. He liked the surroundings and thought it would be an ideal spot for him to build a country home in a place which was so near the city. So he called the real estater and made a quick deal, giving him four times as much as the land and buildings cost him.

"The multimillionaire went right to work. He knocked down the buildings, planted new trees, dug up the filled brook and then, when the place looked again like a farm, he built a comfortable country home for himself and his family.

"When the real estater had sold the land to the millionaire he kept a piece of low ground that the millionaire did not care to have. So after the millionaire had settled himself, the real estater began to think of how to dispose of the remaining piece of ground. It was not suitable for building, but it was an excellent location for a cemetery. So he went to Weiss, the undertaker, and together they organized a new cemetery company, for which they bought some additional land.

"As soon as that millionaire got wind of the kind of neighbors that he was going to get, he sent for the real estater and offered to sell him back his land. The real estater got it back for almost one-fifth of the price that he sold it for. Then he chopped some of the trees, filled up the brook, cut up the land in small lots, and began to build all over again.

"Now you see," Bercovich concluded, "this is real estate. You buy it and you sell it with profit and you buy it back again with more profit. All you need is to get the Indians and have a good friend like me to advise."

"I am glad to hear that you are still my friend," Joe said, grasping his hand. "I have a little money which I would like to invest."

"Don't be in a hurry to invest your money," Berkovich warned, "or some slick fellow will get the best of you. Have patience, Joe. Wait till I come across something good. I have a certain parcel in my mind, a three-family house in Brooklyn, which can be bought very cheap. It is owned by a handsome widow who wants to get married. Ah, you ought to see her, what a fine lady she is! I'll come around and talk to you about it next Sunday."

Joe was expecting him the next Sunday, and I warned Joe I am sure he's got something not so good.

Next time I come to Gonefsky's, Joe was thinking of becoming a real estater himself.

"Just a light lunch? Pickled fish and coffee," Joe repeated to me. Yes, Bercovich the *shadchen,* who became a real estater, was in Gonefsky's again. He came last Wednesday to Joe with all the particulars concerning the three-family house in Brooklyn which the owner, a widow, wants to sell at a great sacrifice.

"Such a house!" Bercovich said; "a regular palace. It is only because the widow needs the money that she sells it so cheap. The house is almost new. It needs only a little repairing and a new coat of paint."

"Are you talking about the widow?" Joe asked.

"No, the house," he said. "And about the widow, I can tell you she is a beautiful young lady. When you look at her you wouldn't believe she is the mother of two children. You'd think she is still a young girl.

"Are you trying to *shadchen* me that widow?" Joe asked Bercovich, becoming a little suspicious.

"Ah, I forgot myself!" And Bercovich began to laugh. "Ha, ha, ha! Such is the force of habit, Joe. Sometimes I think I am still a *shadchen.* But let us go back to business. The house has a first mortgage for $9,000, a second for $5,000, and $4,000 is the price that the widow wants for her share in the property."

And then he went on to show Joe that there is a net profit of $150 a month above the payment of interest, taxes, and all other expenses.

The short of it was that Bercovich and Joe made an appointment to go to Brooklyn Sunday afternoon, when Joe is off, and see that house.

Bercovich left the restaurant about two in the afternoon. In the evening Joe had another visitor, a man he had never seen before.

He had that appearance which made him look like a rabbi, but his beard was trimmed and his manner betrayed him that he was a *shadchen*.

"I am Ziporkes, the well-known *shadchen* from Brownsville," he introduced himself to Joe. "I was once a wealthy real estater, but having lost my fortune in big speculation I became a *shadchen*. Let me have a glass of tea and then we'll have a talk. I came to see you, Mr. Joe, about a party," Mr. Ziporkes said as he squeezed the juice of a slice of lemon in his glass of tea. "She is a beautiful young woman, a widow, and owns a house in Brooklyn. She has two children, but she looks very young, almost girlish. I am sure you will like her."

"In Brooklyn, you say?" Joe asked him, trying to find any connection between his widow and the one of which Bercovich spoke to him.

"Are you trying to sell me the house?" Joe asked him.

"Oh, no!" he said. "It is simply habit. The real estater is talking in me. I am trying to bring you together with a very dear lady who, I am sure, will make you happy."

Joe's head commenced to whirl when he heard this. Here was a difficult problem for him to solve: the lady or the three-family house? One man tempted Joe with a big bargain, the other with a wealthy young widow. Now, which shall it be? To tell the truth he liked the proposition of Mr. Ziporkes' best, for he knew that if he'd marry the widow the house goes with her.

"I tell you, Mr. Ziporkes," Joe said after some thinking,

"I cannot answer until next Monday. At present I have something else in view."

"That's all right," Mr. Ziporkes said. "I can wait. You have some previous proposition, I understand. Good night. I'll see you Monday."

Joe ran to the telephone, called me, and, after explaining, said, "Mr. Shulem, what should I do? I like both propositions."

"Take a look, it can't hurt, but make no commitments," I answered.

At last Sunday came. Bercovich was prompt in keeping his appointment for half-past two. Joe was all dressed up when he came in and they went to Brooklyn.

Joe's heart fluttered when he saw the three-family brick house that was to be his for love or for money.

Soon they were in the house. Five kids who were playing in the hall yelled at the top of their voices:

"Ma! Mr. Bercovich brought us a new papa!"

"Hush, you naughty kids!" Bercovich hollered at them. "Such *momzers!* I tell them just for fun that I am going to bring them a new papa and they take me seriously."

So there were five children, not two as Joe had been told before. Maybe after all Bercovich was a real estater and not a *shadchen.*

Bercovich knocked on a door, up on the second floor. A middle-aged woman opened it and greeted them with a broad smile.

"Mr. Joe Katzman—Mrs. Sarah Kovid," Bercovich introduced them.

Joe looked at the woman—forty she would never see again—and from the manner in which she was dressed up he could see that he was expected not as a prospective buyer of the house, but as a candidate for the lady's hand, heart and children.

They were asked to sit at the table, and there was a usual big spread. Joe began to think over Bercovich's old tricks, how he was trapped many times and how it took courage to get out of the traps. He began to suspect that he was still the same *shadchen* and that his real estate business was only a bluff.

"Well, let us go and take a look over the building," Joe said to Bercovich after some talk.

And as soon as Joe had Bercovich out of the room he said to him:

"Tell me the truth, Mr. Bercovich, are you still a *shadchen* and have you a partner by the name of Ziporkes?"

"Yes," he said, "and I'll be frank with you, Joe, and tell you that I sent him to you in order to help me out in this little scheme, which is for your own good."

"Thank you," Joe said, "now I know it."

As Joe left the house he heard the woman say to Bercovich:

"This is already the sixteenth party you brought here and no result. Think of the expense, with oranges and apples at five and six cents apiece and nuts at twenty-four cents a pound! I guess I'll have to look for another *shadchen*. I think I will call Morris Shulem. He's at least reliable and no monkey business, and he doesn't wear leopard-skin clothes."

16

A Vest for Mr. Pomposh

I wonder if you know Mr. Pomposh, the Rivington street jeweler. He is rich, very rich, although you could never tell it by the clothes he used to wear. If you will search all of New York, you will never find a man who is so negligent in the matter of clothes as Mr. Pomposh was. But in spite of it people liked to deal with him, for he has always been a very honest man.

"Wait until I save up enough money to enable me to retire from business," Mr. Pomposh used to say to me, "and then I'll become a sport, wear nice clothes and have a good time."

However, the more Mr. Pomposh made, the less he cared to retire from business. He lived with his wife, Dora, and their daughter, Betsy, in three rooms behind the jewelry store.

When Betsy graduated from high school she wanted to

attend college. Her father insisted it was a waste of time and money to send a girl to college. "A boy can learn to be a doctor or a lawyer or maybe an accountant, but a girl, she should get a job and look for a husband."

Mr. Pomposh was from the old school and he felt that all women should be like his wife—help wait on trade in the store, keep house and cook her three meals for her family. For Dora to keep house it was very easy, for the Pomposhes had practically no furniture. However, Betsy had different ideas.

When Betsy was denied the right of a rich man's daughter to go to college, she conspired with her mother to have her father send her to business college.

The business college got Betsy a job in a big insurance company's office after she completed her six months' secretarial course.

One evening when Betsy came home from work she found me talking to her father in the store. Just then a couple came in and Betsy took the liberty to say to me, "Mr. Shulem, would you like a cup of coffee or a glass of tea? Those people will keep Papa busy for a long time. They are engaged and they can't make up their minds whether to buy an engagement ring or furniture."

"I'm always happy to talk to you. I've known you since you were born," I said proudly, following the young lady into the combination kitchen, dining room and parlor. "Tell me," I continued. "What did you want to talk to me about? Are you maybe thinking about getting married?"

"Mr. Shulem, only to you can I talk," Betsy said quietly. "Mama is under the finger of Papa. I met a fine boy in the office where I work. His father is the comptroller of the company and some day he will be a big man with the insurance company. But how can I invite him here? And the way Papa and Mama dress? Just like *shleppers!* Can you get Papa to buy at least a new suit and maybe we can get a flat not behind the store?"

"That's a big order," I said. "But don't worry. Shulem the *shadchen* will find a way."

One day, quite a change came over Mr. Pomposh. While passing Canal Street he saw in the window of a gents' furnishing store a white vest with yellow stripes and it was marked "89¢ cut down from $2.75."

"That means a dollar eighty-six cents saved," he said to himself, and he entered the store and bought the vest.

When he came home he showed the vest to Mrs. Pomposh, and she liked it too.

"Now people will not say I am stingy," he said to his wife. But Dora suggested:

"I was thinking how much nicer you would look if you would only have a better shirt and a fancy necktie to go with that vest."

"Perhaps you are right," Mr. Pomposh replied, and the same day he bought a shirt and tie. I happened to drop in just at the time when Mr. Pomposh was standing before a mirror, in the back of his jewelry shop, trying on his new shirt and tie.

"Well, what do you think of me now?" he boasted.

"I think you need a new suit of clothes," I said, remembering part of Betsy's worry.

"Mr. Shulem is right," Mrs. Pomposh said approvingly. "No wonder people think he is a very wise man, besides being a good *shadchen*."

Mr. Pomposh thought hard, and then he said:

"Not so soon. All this is too much for one day. I'll first buy a new hat and a new pair of shoes."

I went with him to help him buy. "It is a long time since I bought a hat or a pair of shoes," he said, "and I forgot how."

Next day he came to me, saying: "Mr. Shulem, I'm giving you a lot of trouble, but you are an old family friend. Your father and my father—*aleihem hasholem*—were neighbors in the old country, and very good neighbors at that. So please, come with me and help me select a suit of clothes. Before it was not noticeable, but now, with my new hat, new shoes, new shirt, new tie and fancy vest, my clothes are conspicuous. Please come with me."

I had a time in getting him that suit, for Mr. Pomposh wanted the best for the least money. At last he got one, a dark blue and of the latest cut.

I tell you, he looks like a new man. People who come to his store do not know him. "Where is Mr. Pomposh?" they ask. "Did he sell out, and are you the new proprietor?"

Of course Mr. Pomposh is delighted. One day—it is a week after he bought the suit of clothes—he said to his wife:

"Dora, we ought to live in better rooms. Let us take a flat around here, or even on Grand Street. Betsy is grown up now and we should have a nice place for her to entertain her friends."

"But how can we move to a nice house," the woman argued, "when we haven't got one decent chair or decent table or even a couch? Before we move in we have to get new furniture."

"Furniture, furniture," he repeated. "That means at least five hundred dollars, and we'll have to pay high rent besides."

I lost much time in helping him to select his furniture, but how could I help it? Can you refuse a favor to a *landsman* whose father and your father were neighbors? And besides, there was Betsy.

The flat was rented and the new furniture delivered. After everything was put in place, the parlor looked like a bridegroom in full dress, but without a collar and tie, while the dining room looked like a bride who was barefoot.

And then Mr. Pomposh began to talk of giving a party and getting a *choson* for Betsy.

Betsy was excited about the party and informed her parents that she was almost going steady with a fine successful young man, and right then and there a date was set for the Pomposhes' first party.

"And what will I wear?" Mrs. Pomposh asked.

"You too, Dora!" the jeweler exclaimed.

"Your wife is right," I added. "She must appear decent. How do you expect her to show herself in her old dress before your friends and Betsy's intended, who will surely come dressed in their best?"

Mr. Pomposh, weakening every day, gave in. Dora got a new dress, a coat, a hat and who knows what else?

"The same Dora," Mr. Pomposh remarked when his wife appeared before him in her new clothes. "The same *yente,* only in a different dress."

The party was given, Betsy's intended proposed, and the guests could not get over the change in the life of the Pomposh family. Why, they lived too swell, even for Grand Street!

Only one thing was still missing in their house. A servant. Mrs. Pomposh overheard Betsy's intended's mother make a remark about that.

Dora told it to her husband.

"Since we made up our minds to live in style, why not get a girl?" she asked.

"But girls are very expensive nowadays," he argued. "And what will a girl do here?"

His arguments were to no avail. Mrs. Pomposh got the girl. This was her first step toward independence. After that Mrs. Pomposh began to buy new dresses, new hats and shoes, until Mr. Pomposh cursed the day he bought that yellow striped fancy vest for eighty-nine cents, and last Monday he came to me and said:

"Mr. Shulem. I have given you a lot of trouble for nothing. Betsy got married without a *shadchen*. Now I'll give you a chance to make some money on me. I have decided to get a new wife."

17

A Shadchen's Life Is Not a Happy One

Years ago, when I was in the peddling business, I had an ambition to be a politician. In fact, I took the first step in that direction. I bought a Cremo cigar. To this day I still smoke a cigar, and once in a while, when I light up, I think of my dreams of the old days of being a politician. I have always liked to help people and I feel that part of the job of being a politician, like a *shadchen*, is to help people.

I still remember the politician who would come around and check my pushcart license; he always wore a double-breasted suit with of course a handkerchief in his breast pocket that matched his tie and he smoked a cigar. One day I asked him how to be in politics and he said, "You got a better racket and you don't have to eat those dried-over chicken dinners at five bucks a throw." Then, when I was young, I did not understand, but today I do.

Some people think to be a politician is a soft job. Other people think that to be a *shadchen* is the same as a politician, but they are wrong. In either case one has to stand a good deal of *tzoris* before he accomplishes anything.

Let me illustrate.

One of the *shadchen*'s duties is attending many public affairs, banquets especially. It is all right to go to banquets once or twice or even three times a week, but what would you do if you had to attend three banquets in one night?

That was exactly what happened to me about a month ago. One banquet was given in honor of a synagogue president who retired after twenty-five years of faithful service; the other was in celebration of the tenth anniversary of my lodge; and the third was in honor of a city official who got in some trouble with his superiors, and he needed something to show that at least the people of the East Side were on his side.

Since I found it necessary to attend all three, I said to my wife: "Minnie, we do it like this. We'll go to one banquet and stay for the *marinierte* herring or chopped liver appetizer and for the soup. Then we will go to the second and partake of a piece of broiled chicken with salad and olives. At last we will go to the third and finish our meal."

Minnie liked the idea. "You are a real smarty, my husband," she told me. "No wonder people respect you."

The idea was practical, no one will deny, yet it failed.

We first went to the banquet of my lodge. We found everybody there but two speakers—one a rabbi, the other an alderman, who were invited to speak, and the arrangement committee would not allow us to start with the dinner before the speakers arrived. So we waited and waited, and when it was ten o'clock and no food in sight, I said to my wife: "Minnie, let us go. If we start now for the other banquet we will be able to get some broiled chicken and salad, and maybe we will stay for the next course."

As we came to the place of the second banquet, where the city official was being honored for his faithful and efficient service to the city and his constituents, the dinner was at the end and nothing was left but a small cup of black coffee and some ices, but we could not even get that, for it was speech time. The guest of honor was being praised, toasted and acclaimed as the best servant of the people and as a model of purity in politics. Minnie later told me she overheard one remark in a whisper, "Nothing will help him, for the evidence is strong against him."

I took a look at the program and saw that nine more speakers were on the printed list to speak, which meant at least a dozen more speakers, because at the last minute the guest of honor always brings in two or three last-minute speakers that were too late to give their names to the printer. I leaned over to Minnie and suggested: "Minnie, if we hurry up and leave we can make the synagogue affair."

As we arrived at the third banquet we found everybody leaving the tables. They were already through with the dinner and the speeches.

"You came just in time, Mr. Shulem," said Mr. Mandel, the real estater, but I did not appreciate the sarcasm, because Minnie and I were hungry.

"Yes, just in time," he repeated. "I was expecting you all evening. I spent more time looking at the door for you than I did in listening to the speeches. I have some business to talk over with you. Are you listening?"

"I'm listening," I answered.

"You see," he began. "You know my oldest daughter, the schoolteacher. Well—Bella, she is a marriageable girl and she is very particular in her choice. Once we thought that she will never find a man to suit her taste but lately she commences to keep company with a fine gentleman. He seems a little older than she, but otherwise. . . ."

"So, what do you want me to do?" I asked. "Your daughter has got a man without my help."

"Mr. Shulem, you are not in good humor tonight," Mr. Mandel remarked, looking and wondering. "You never used to talk that way. Maybe you overate at another banquet? Sure, I want your help. I want you to investigate a certain young man, and if you think he is all right, you have a chance to earn a *shadchen* fee."

"So how long have they been keeping company?" I asked in a business-like tone.

"Only a few weeks," Mrs. Mandel broke in, "and although he once visited her in our house, I have reason to believe that they often meet outside somewhere. Last week Bella received a letter, and she looked so happy when she read it that we are sure it was from a man. Then a man called on her and they had a long talk in the parlor. Next day she received a big box of candy and a card on the package said it was 'Compliments of Mr. Krantzkuchen, of 1500 Grand Street.' Now, it is up to you to go and find out all about him."

At the house of that address I found an old lady who was very busy baking. Mr. Krantzkuchen was out, she told me, but he was expected back very soon.

"All right," I said to the old lady. "I'll go now and come back in an hour, and if he comes in the meantime, please tell him that Shulem the *shadchen* was here."

"What does he need a *shadchen* for?" the old woman asked with a surprised look. "He is already married and a father of four children, and I am his mother-in-law."

"Oh, then it is not Mr. Krantzkuchen," I said; "but it must be his younger brother, the one that's keeping company with a schoolteacher."

"There is only one Mr. Krantzkuchen in this house," the mother-in-law fired at me, "and he has no brothers."

The old woman then ran to a bedroom and I heard her talk rapidly:

"*Oy!* My poor Jenny! Charlie is keeping company with a schoolteacher. He intends to get a divorce. There is a *shadchen. . . .*"

The rest I did not wait to hear, for I ran for the door and went quickly downstairs. It is not a pleasant thing to meet a woman at the moment she discovers that her husband is keeping company with another woman.

What was I to do now? Of course I had to go over to the Mandels and tell them the truth.

When I came to the house no one was there but Bella the schoolteacher, who was helping the cook make *gefillte* fish.

"What a nice girl," I said to myself, "and she is about to fall in the hands of a wily man. I must save her."

"Good afternoon, Miss Mandel!" I greeted her as I came in. "The *gefillte* fish you are making teases my palate just to look at. How happy will be the man who will eat your fish every *Shabbos!*"

"Man, man, man!" she mimicked me, "you *shadchens* have no other subject but man, man, man. I hate men! It is a sad world indeed that eventually a girl has got to take a man. To me all men seem so silly, not much wiser than my pupils in school. I tell you that I would rather spend all my life with the little pupils than give it away to a big one."

"Miss Mandel," I began, not knowing exactly how to proceed, "is it possible that there is not one man in the world that would suit your taste?"

"So far I have not met one," she answered.

"But at the same time," I continued, "I advise you as a

friend of your family to look out for Mr. Krantzkuchen. He is a married man and a father of four children."

"I know that," she said, "and the oldest boy is a pupil of my class. He was the worst kid in the neighborhood, but I changed him. Now he is a well-behaved little gentleman. His father is so grateful to me that he is showering me with presents. Why should I be suspicious of him? Mr. Shulem, I'm afraid you have been misinformed."

"I think so, too," I admitted with rue.

Now you see how much a *shadchen* has to stand in connection with his profession.

Maybe I should have been a politician!

18

August

It is another typical August Monday, hot and humid. Even the fans are tired, they blow nothing.

All of my better clients are on vacation. New York, it is empty. The papers have a headline: almost two million people at Coney Island.

At times a *shadchen* is like a coat manufacturer. Seasons. A rich man's daughter likes to get married in the summer, a middle-income person usually gets married in the spring or fall, and the so-so income gets married in the winter. I don't know why but if you look into the marriage picture you'll see it works out that way. I have found, if I plan my introducing parties on a seasonal basis I get better results.

August is in-between seasons.

I remember one August, as the weather was so hot in the city, I thought it would be best for me to go and join the crowd at Arverne. "Maybe," I said to my wife, "I can pick up a little business out there."

But I ought to know better. A *shadchen* like me, with so many years of experience, ought to know better. The seashore is no place for making matches. Mothers who take out their girls to the seashore with the hope of catching husbands for them should take this tip from me, the old reliable Shulem, that unless their girls can win on their natural merits only, they should not dare to bring them out there. A girl with a poor shape and an unattractive complexion should go to a place where she can keep her physical imperfections under cover.

So I left Arverne-by-the-Sea and went to Tannersville, in the mountains. Here was I again disappointed. Plenty of nice-looking girls, also a $20,000 widow, but very few young men in the place. And the few that were there flirted with the married women.

It makes me unhappy to see the Monday to Friday romances between the unmarried bachelors and the married women, who become faithful wives when their husbands come up for the weekend. And the wives. When you come to one of these mountain resorts you cannot tell the difference between a mother of seven children and a seventeen-year-old, they dress so much alike. And no wonder that the married men flirt too, when they are free from pinochle.

One day I met there a young couple who stopped at a neighboring hotel. They were Mr. and Mrs. Archibald Kanovitz, who were married through me about eight years before, and now they had their four children with them.

Let me tell you how they got married before I go further.

He was a drummer in the ladies' dress-trimmings line,

just at the beginning of his career. I don't think he made more than $30 a week, while she was a daughter of well-to-do parents, and $30 a week was just pin money to her. But they loved each other very much, and who can stand before love and a *shadchen?* And he was a bright young man, so her parents, after arguments, agreed to let their daughter marry him, and they took him in their real estate business.

A week before the wedding Kanovitz comes to me and says:

"Mr. Shulem, I am wanting to ask a favor of you. Just now I was in my *machuton*'s house and I saw so many presents coming from the family on the bride's side. I am very much ashamed as my own family is being very poor. You know I have no parents. I would like to get presents from an aunt and cousins that I have in Brownsville, and as they are too poor to send any presents, I would like for you to send something in their name. Here is some money."

He gave me the name of his aunt and also his four cousins. And two days later, the bride received a fine silver bread tray and a half dozen silver spoons, with the compliments and best wishes of Archibald Kanovitz's aunt and his four cousins.

The next thing that Kanovitz asks is to send a telegram, in the name of his aunt and cousins, on the day of the wedding, informing that they were unable to come, as they have to catch a steamer for Bermuda.

All is forgotten until a month after the wedding—that is, after the newlyweds had returned from their honeymoon trip.

They found a letter which is addressed to both Mr. and Mrs. Kanovitz, and the bride, seeing it first, opened and read it, something like this:

My dear Nephew:

First of all let me wish you *mazel tov* from the bottom of my heart. It is too bad that I am so poor that I could not be invited and send you a wedding present, not even an alarm clock. But "poverty is no disgrace" as people say, and so I am very happy that you my dear nephew had fallen into such fortune, by marrying a girl from wealthy parents; good luck to you both! Now don't forget your poor aunt, who is struggling very hard for a living. If you can send me a few dollars this week it would help to pay my rent.

Mr. Kanovitz was plenty embarrassed after making such a bluff about his aunt and cousins. But as the bride and her parents loved him, they made a joke of the business and forgave him.

All that had happened eight years before. I tell all those details to show you how ungrateful some men are, for on the second day after I met them again in Tannersville, I found Kanovitz in the drugstore entertaining three of the fanciest ladies of the hotel. The ladies had more on their faces than on their bodies.

"It does not mean that I love my wife less," Kanovitz excused himself later, when I gently reproached him on his misconduct. I was really surprised to see him in the company of those women, who were much less beautiful than his own wife.

In the evening, after supper, I went over to the hotel where Mr. Kanovitz and his family were stopping, but he had already gone, Mrs. Kanovitz told me, and she did not know where.

She took a walk with me and confided that she thought her husband went out for an automobile ride with the Garfinkel woman, who was extremely tall, with red hair and a freckled face.

"I am sure of my Archibald," she told me, "that he does not in any way forget that he is a gentleman and a father of four children, but I am tired of the whispers around me and the pitying looks that I meet around here. I am sure he is not guilty of any real wrong. Perhaps if I would make up my face and dress like those women do he would stick to me all the time. Men are so funny."

"Why don't you try it," I dared her.

"Should I?" she asked laughing. "Well, I must try."

Next evening a barn dance was given in the village for the benefit of a sanitarium. All the ladies came dressed in their best or their worst. Their hair was made up in the latest fashion. Mrs. Kanovitz, who came alone, is also there, as she was sure her husband would not miss the affair.

I watched her from a corner. Her cheeks were painted a deep red and she had about a can of powder on her neck and shoulders, which were bare. The men who knew her came up, complimented her that she never looked so beautiful as on that evening.

At last Mr. Kanovitz noticed her. He was greatly surprised at the way she fixed herself up and at her presence at the barn dance. As I saw him coming toward her, I moved nearer, too.

All of a sudden Kanovitz's face became angry, and coming up to his wife, he said in a low but desperate tone:

"Fanny, go home quick, wash off that paint from your face and put on decent clothes. I would never permit my wife, the mother of my children, to show herself in public like this!"

Men are funny—and so is the month of August.

19

The Rose of Delancey Street

I would like to advertise in the newspaper telling about my *shadchen* business. These newspapers are in competition with me. They print "Advice to the Lovelorn" which tells people what to do in such matters. Lately the papers are printing notices in the Want Ad sections and for free on how to meet a mate. A *shadchen*'s life is not a bed of roses.

"Excuse me—but I was so busy reading the matrimonial column in the *Daily Eagle* that I didn't see you come in," said Joe Katzman. "Tea and a Danish? Is that all? Oh, I see by your vest that you were at a banquet last night."

This matrimonial column is competition. Maybe it could be a splendid idea. But I think a person still needs a *shadchen* to handle details.

If you are single and lonesome just write a letter to the editor, give him a full description of yourself, describe your ideal of a wife, or a husband—as the case may be—and your letter will be printed in the paper, free, without any cost. Of course, you are not to sign your real name to it, but just something like "Lonesome Joe," "Bashful Abe," "Sentimental Sarah," or "Pining Becky." Those who will find interest in your letter will advertise for your right name and address and for more information.

Joe Katzman, a waiter at Gonefsky's Ten Course Café and Restaurant decided to answer an ad, and he said:

"Mr. Shulem, I have been reading this 'do-it-yourself' *shadchen* business in the paper and I think it is genuine, for no one could write such a letter for fun. Listen to this. I have the clipping in my pocket for a week already.

Dear Editor:

I am a young woman of thirty. My friends tell me I am very beautiful, and I am in good health. I am a dressmaker, having my own establishment and earning about $15,000 a year. I enjoy all the pleasures of life. I go to shows, operas and take automobile rides, paying my own way. I am very much satisfied with myself and the world. But there are times when I feel lonesome, sometimes even miserable. And that is because I am all alone in the world, all alone in my beautiful flat.

Once I was married, but my marriage was a failure. I was a young girl then, innocent and inexperienced with the ways of men. I trusted myself in the hands of a man who did not know how to appreciate a kind and loving wife. After we married he spent his nights going to meetings or hung around cigar stores. I used to spend my evenings all alone, just the same as I do now. So I decided to leave him, buying my freedom for a big price. I had to give up half of my savings of many years.

For a time I thought that I would never care to marry

again, but of late I began to yearn for companionship, for friendship, for love.

I don't ask for much. My ideal is a plain young man of about my age, who will appreciate a true and affectionate wife and help me to maintain a happy home, where love and sunshine will reign supreme.

The Rose of Delancey Street

"Well, what do you think of such a letter, Mr. Shulem?" Joe asked me. "Here is the one who was destined for me from heaven. I advertised for her address and I got a note from her sent to Box 204 in the office of the *Eagle*. 'For a time,' she wrote to me, 'you are to send me your letters in care of Mr. Shmulevitz, who is my uncle, at the address below.' I understood that she wanted to get some more information about me before allowing me to call on her in person.

"I kept corresponding with her and I got some nice answers. Her letters were full of sentiment and encouragement. 'Maybe some day we shall know each other better and be more than friends,' she wrote to me in one of her letters. In another letter she wrote, 'I am a size 42.' I wrote to her daily; she wrote only once every other day. In one of her last letters she said that she hoped we'd be able to meet and see each other very soon.

"One evening I went to the wedding of my cousin, Ben, who is the ticket taker in Borishevsky's theater. And there, in the center of the hall, was standing Bercovich the *shadchen,* talking to two pretty girls and fondling his chin in a dignified manner.

"This time I was not afraid to meet him. On the contrary, I wanted to talk to him. I had a great desire to show him that I was about to be a do-it-yourself *shadchen.* I had eight letters the 'Rose of Delancey Street' had written to me in my pocket, as evidence.

"So when the ceremony was over and the guests sat down at the tables, I did not mind it at all when that Bercovich came over and invited himself to sit next to me.

" 'I am glad to see you, Joe, and in a happy mood, for a change,' he said.

" 'Yes, Mr. Bercovich,' I said, 'I am happy, for I am going to be engaged pretty soon to a nice young lady with a big business.'

" 'She is a dressmaker; I know her,' Bercovich said coolly.

" 'Look here, Mr. Bercovich,' I said pointing my finger right in his eyes. 'You are not going to get a penny for this match. It is of no use for you to butt in. This is a self-made do-it-myself match. Here I have already eight letters from her.' And so I took the bunch of letters from my pocket, counting them, 'One, two, three, four, five, six, seven, eight.'

" 'And I have yours,' that *shadchen,* said, taking out a bunch of letters from his pocket and counting them. 'One, two, three, four, five,' and up to seventeen.

"They were my letters; I recognized them. I was so angry at myself that I was ready to call myself fool, idiot.

" 'Remember, Joe, you are at a wedding,' the *shadchen* warned me. 'Your angry face is attracting the attention of the other guests. Let us talk business now. Tell me, what reason have you to be angry at me? With the eugenists on one side and the matrimonial column in the *Eagle* on the other side, how are we *shadchens* going to do business? Don't you think that the world owes us a living? Seeing how the papers are trying to ruin a profession, I decided to steal their powder, as they say, and make use of their matrimonial column to help me in my *gesheft.*'

" 'But who is the Rose of Delancey Street?' I asked.

" 'There are many of them,' Bercovich answered. 'You can pick them by the hundreds, by the thousands, in the garden of Delancey Street.'

" 'The Rose of Delancey Street is no lie, but she is a composite type,' Bercovich continued. 'I have taken separate qualities of various girls and combined them in one grand ideal. There is a dressmaker on my list, but she does not earn $15,000 a year. There is a girl who earns $30 a week, but she would marry a doctor or a lawyer only. There is still another girl who is lonesome and would marry anybody, but she is neither a dressmaker nor does she make $15,000 a year. She is a girl over forty and works as a cook. The flat where she works is really beautiful, but her missus is very mean. How about meeting the cook?'

" 'Mr. Bercovich,' I said, 'please leave me alone. Don't even talk to me.'

" 'Joe,' said Bercovich, 'I promise no more tricks, just let me be your *shadchen*. And to show you my heart's in the right place, I'll cut my fee from ten per cent to nine per cent only because of the *tzoris* I caused you.'

" 'And to show you I mean business, too,' " said I, " 'make it eight per cent and I'll stop watering your coffee.' "

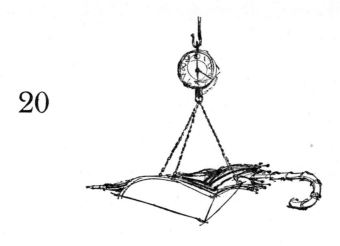

20

Edelstein's Dilemma

Many times have I walked on the street and met and said hello to our next-door neighbors, who unfortunately are deaf people. These people talk and hear with their fingers and I always marvel at them. And good lip readers, too. But what if they should turn their head, just for a second? They could lose an important argument or the answer to an important question. It could be a perplexing problem.

Oftentimes young people in love come to me and reveal the aches and pains of their hearts. And Shulem the *shadchen* is always glad to help them. I sometimes wonder what would love be without a *shadchen*.

About a year ago a fine young man who was a little hard of hearing came up to my house and told me a story of love and woe, of such a kind that no writer of love stories could have ever invented. I tell you I am reading all the *bubba monsis* in the daily papers and I have never read of a peculiar happening like the one told to me by Mr. Ralph Waldo Edelstein.

Mr. Edelstein had been keeping company with a very pretty girl for two years. She was exceptionally kind to him and took great care in not making him feel his physical defect, for sometimes people of that sort are a little sensitive. She was the only person in whose presence he felt free to talk as much as he desired, and he was very happy in her company.

On the second anniversary of their acquaintance he braces himself and puts the question to her whether she would like to marry him.

"I saw her smile," he told me, "and I saw her lips move slightly, but I could not hear what she said."

"But, of course," I added, "if you had watched carefully the movement of her lips, you could judge whether she said 'yes' or 'no.'"

"Yes, I did watch her lips closely, and yet I could not make out whether it was 'yes' or 'no,'" he said. "It seems to me that what she said was neither 'yes' nor 'no,' but something quite different."

That was indeed a puzzle. If neither "yes" nor "no" what then could it be?

"And I tried many ways to find out," Mr. Edelstein continued. "As I came home I asked my mother whether there was any milk in the house, and I looked in her face, watching how her lips would move saying yes or no, but she merely said, 'I'll see,' and going over to the refrigerator, she got the milk for me."

I became greatly interested, and my sympathy for the young man was growing all the time.

"Did you try any other way?" I asked.

"Yes," he answered. "I went to the fruit store on our

corner and I asked the owner if he had any ch
watched him very carefully, expecting him to ans\
the affirmative or in the negative, but his ans
'Peanuts only.' You hear people say 'yes' and 'no
times a day, but just when you want to hear on
words you cannot get them to say it."

"Now, suppose you try me," I volunteered.

"Oh, thank you," he smiled, "but I already had
to hear these words spoken by my niece, a little
girl, just two years old. I took her on my lap this
and I asked her if she loved me and she said 'ye
I asked her if she would go home with me and the l
said 'no.' And now I am almost sure that Frances sa
thing different from 'yes' or 'no.' Mr. Shulem, I
know what to do with myself. I just can't call on
again, not knowing whether I was accepted or re

"Well," I said hesitatingly, "you need not worry.
the *shadchen* has handled greater troubles than y
will be all right. You see, after all, the *shadchen* is t
person to arrange matches. I'll see your Frances
as I find time."

"But what will you tell her?" my new client wo

"Just leave that to me," I said. "She will never kn
you spoke to me of your predicament. Just leave
Shulem."

That same evening I called on the young lady.
she heard that I was a *shadchen* she began to laug
said:

"Why, I already have a beau and I'm as good as en
to him."

" 'As good' does not mean that you are really enga
I said, "so would you like to listen to other propositi

"I don't want to listen to any other propositions,'

129

answered curtly. "The one who loves me is the best man in the world."

"But there may be one who is still better," I argued. "For instance, a young gentleman like Ralph Waldo Edelstein, who—"

She did not let me finish my sentence.

"He's my beau! He proposed to me last night and I promised to marry him!" she exclaimed. "And you didn't know it? Mr. Shulem, please go and see Ralph and ask him if he would like to marry a girl by the name of Frances Goldin? Oh, that will be great fun, I wish I could see his face!"

"I'm going right now," I said.

Of course Mr. Edelstein was very happy when I told him of the conversation between his sweetheart and myself, and how she refused to listen to me, thinking I was offering her another young man.

"And yet," he said thoughtfully, after several minutes passed, "I cannot understand what she did say when I asked her to marry me. It could not have been 'no' and yet I am sure it was not 'yes,' either. Mr. Shulem, I have missed the most important word in a man's life."

"But now you can ask her," I answered.

"Oh, no," he blushed. "I'd be ashamed to ask her. Maybe some day."

"Why should that bother your head at all?" I wondered. "Why should you care? Be happy and forget it!"

Two months later they were married, and after their wedding I did not see either of them until last week, when Mr. Edelstein suddenly turned up.

It was a rainy day—just the kind of a day a *shadchen* stays home. I was sitting reading a newspaper and smoking a cigar which I got at a swell wedding, when my wife came in, announcing that a Mr. Edelstein wants to see me.

"Edelstein, Edelstein," I repeated to myself, "the name sounds familiar; let him come in."

As he entered my office, I recognized in him the same Mr. Ralph Waldo Edelstein whom I helped out of his peculiar dilemma almost a year ago.

"Well, well! What a guest!" I greeted him. "And what is the good news?"

"I just dropped in to tell you something of great interest," he began. "I know now what was the answer my Frances gave me when I asked her to marry me a year ago."

"You know it already? Then please tell me!" I begged him.

"She said: 'Well, well—at last!' That is what she said!"

It seems to me now that a woman can say "yes" in many more ways than one.

21

Sadie's Secret of Success

It happened some time ago, and the Kretchmer family was one of my first clients. I was a *shadchen* just a short time, so that is why I am putting it down in my chronicles for the benefit of future historians and also *shadchens*.

Abraham Kretchmer, the wholesale grocer, was a father of six daughters, the youngest already being of marriageable age. There came a time I offered him two parties to choose from for his eldest, Sadie: a doctor who wanted $10,000, and an engineer who maybe was willing to settle for $5,000.

"If you please, Mr. Shulem," Mr. Kretchmer said, "maybe can you get me a doctor who is a little bit of an engineer?"

"Your stinginess will cost you dearly," I warned him. As time passed he began to regret that he let pass such good chances. He kept his younger girls in short dresses, with their braids hanging down, like schoolgirls, in order not to betray the age of his Sadie, who had said good-by to thirty.

One day comes Mr. Kretchmer to my office, looking very sad, and says:

"Mr. Shulem, please do something for me. Can you imagine the feelings of a father when he passes through his home and he sees petticoats here, corsets there, and dresses and stockings and shoes in every closet, nook and corner? Have pity? Help me to get rid of my department store. But first help me to get rid of my Sadie."

"You could have been playing with your grandchildren today," I said to him, "if you had made up your mind that time, either on the doctor or on the engineer."

"But what is the use of spilling salt on my wounds?" Mr. Kretchmer wailed. "Do something. Or give me an advice what can I do. As soon as a young man finally comes to see Sadie, and he sees Rachel, the girl next to her, he wants to talk and maybe marry the younger one, Rachel, and not Sadie."

"And Rachel? What does she do?" I asked.

"She does everything to attract the young man's attention, and she does it out of revenge, because I make her wear children's dresses. All of my girls are not liking it."

"I'll tell you what you can do," I said to him after giving the matter some thought, "and if you follow my advice you will get rid of Sadie pretty soon. Let Rachel be the oldest girl for a while and Sadie be the younger."

"What do you mean?" he asked.

"Mr. Kretchmer," I explain, "can't you understand a simple thing like that? Rachel wants to wear a long skirt and otherwise to dress like a grown-up girl. Let her do it.

And have Sadie put on a short dress and let her braids hang down her back."

"And then?"

"Mr. Kretchmer, why can't you understand? Then Rachel will be the older girl and Sadie her younger sister. You see?"

"At last," he finally said, his face breaking into a smile.

After the matter had been arranged between the girls I came to Mr. Kretchmer's house, bringing a party with me, a nice young man, whose father was in the wholesale egg business.

The young man I brought for Rachel, who was acting as the eldest. Rachel was expecting him and she was dressed up in her sister's long dress.

As soon as the couple were introduced and they began to talk, Sadie, who was wearing now a short dress, entered and butted in, playing with her long braid.

In the beginning, Charles Blank, the egg merchant's son, was annoyed, but soon he began to turn his attentions from Rachel to Sadie. Seeing that my plan was beginning to work, I made a sign to Mr. Kretchmer, who ordered Sadie out of the parlor.

"A young girl like you," he said, "ought to stay in the kitchen and help mother to prepare refreshments for our guests."

Sadie left the parlor, where the conversation took place, but not before throwing a loving little side glance at the young man.

After that glance the young man's speech started to lag, and he could hardly keep up the conversation with Rachel. He was looking toward the door, expecting Sadie to come back.

In a few minutes, when she returned, his face became radiant, and he regained his power of speech.

That night young Mr. Blank told me his secret, that he had fallen in love with Sadie. It was love at first sight, he told me. The moment he saw her he felt a dart in his heart. He could not explain it, but he felt that Sadie was the only woman for him.

"But," I protested, "this is not right. Mr. Kretchmer will not allow Sadie to marry before he marries off Rachel."

"Then I'll wait for her," he said. "Please talk to Sadie's father for me. I think I want to marry her!"

"But," I said, "the chances are that when her father will hear that you have changed your mind, he will forbid you to come to his house."

"Then I'll meet her outside the house," he said resolutely. "Love will find a way."

Next morning I ran over to Mr. Kretchmer to tell him the good news. Before I could say a word he flashed a letter in my face.

"Sadie received this love letter from Mr. Blank this morning. He writes that he must see her and asks her to meet him this afternoon at the Mazeltov Photoplay Theatre."

"Mazeltov Photoplay Theatre?" I said. "This is a good place. Let them meet and by all means let them elope. The sooner, the better."

Two weeks later they quietly left together and were married in Jersey, after which they came to Mr. Kretchmer, asking his forgiveness and his blessings, which he gave them.

I merely asked for my check, and I got it, too.

22

The Heart Specialist

I have a number of doctors and lawyers on my clients' list and usually I like to push lawyers. But, since Belkin the lawyer played a mean trick on me, cheating me out of my rightful and hard-earned fee, I changed my mind. Now, I would not wish my worst enemy to have business with lawyers. And as for myself, I would at any time rather have dealings with ten doctors than with one lawyer.

Here is how it happened:

Once I received a card from a widow by the name of Mrs. Silberblatt, who lives in the Bronx, asking me to call on her. I had heard of the lady before, and I knew she had a marriageable daughter and plenty of money, just the kind of people a *shadchen* likes to deal with. So I called on her the same day I received her card.

Mrs. Silberblatt came directly to the point saying, "I

would like for my daughter Evelyn a doctor with a well-established practice. Have you got one?"

Since she was so forward I decided to use forward language. "How much is the *nadan?*" I have always felt delicate discussions of the heart should be talked over gently. I was slightly embarrassed.

But just as coldly as I spoke she answered me, "Six thousand in cash, besides a well-furnished flat."

"I have a doctor with a good income," I said, looking in my notebook, "but you can't get him for less than $15,000. Not one cent. He is a heart specialist and has a great future before him. You have heard of Dr. Fliegenose."

"That's the kind of man I would want for my Evelyn," the widow said, "but I could not give him any more than what I said. My money is all tied up in real estate and I wouldn't sell my property now. The market is—how you say—soft and if I sell I take a loss. But if the doctor would only meet my Evelyn, he would fall in love with her and would take anything as long as he gets her."

"Maybe," I said, for Evelyn was a real beauty and had beautiful long blond hair.

"I'll tell you what I'll do," Mrs. Silberblatt said after thinking a little while. "I am going to call the doctor and ask him to examine my heart. Meanwhile he will meet Evelyn, and then you will do the rest."

I agreed to that and left the house.

Dr. Fliegenose called that evening and he found that Mrs. Silberblatt's heart was greatly affected, but he undertook to cure her. He was then introduced to Evelyn, in a professional way, and right away he became interested in her heart too. He found that she was also showing signs of her mother's ailment.

To make a long story short, the doctor became a frequent caller. Mrs. Silberblatt was delighted, and so was the druggist on the corner. But at the end of the month the doctor sent in a bill for fourteen visits at the rate of $10 each, and underneath the bill was pasted a slip, "Please remit."

As soon as Mrs. Silberblatt received the doctor's bill she telephoned me and said, "I am willing to give Dr. Fliegenose $10,000, for I see he knows his business. Now you talk to him right away."

But in the meantime the doctor had raised the price on himself to $20,000, as his practice has lately been increased.

"Maybe you would like to get a lawyer for your daughter?" I asked Mrs. Silberblatt. "I have a lawyer who has good connections and I'm sure some day he will be a judge."

"And how much?" the widow asked me.

"He also wants $15,000," I said. "But you know lawyers, you can always make a deal. Maybe if he would see your daughter he would take $12,000 or maybe even $10,000. Could you think up some reason for calling him? Any business troubles?"

"Business troubles I have none, thank God," she said, "but I could ask him to come and write a will. The lawyer's name?"

"Alexander Belkin," I said. "I'll contact him today and have him call you."

"Please use the telephone and call him right now," said Mrs. Silberblatt.

The same evening Mr. Belkin came to see Mrs. Silberblatt and she commenced to tell him how she intended to dispose of her money and real estate after her death, and the lawyer made notes, promising to call again with the will made out in the proper legal form.

"Tell me," I asked Mrs. Silberblatt when I called on her the next day, "what were the terms of the will you dictated?"

"Oh," she said laughing, "I gave nearly everything to Evelyn, except $5,000 each for my three sons, $3,000 for charity and $5,000 more for some poor relatives. Evelyn's share is to be over $75,000."

"Well, that will surely catch him," I said.

"I hope so," the widow answered, lifting her eyes to the ceiling, as if praying to heaven.

Five days later I called again at Mrs. Silberblatt's house.

"*Nu?*" I asked. "Are we going to have an engagement party?"

"I can't understand him," Mrs. Silberblatt said thoughtfully. "Every day he calls, spends most of his time with me, and does not even pay the slightest attention to Evelyn."

"And the will?" I asked.

"He seems to have forgotten that there was a will to be made out," Mrs. Silberblatt answered.

Is it necessary for me to tell you the end? A month later the lawyer and the widow were engaged.

But when I claimed my fee, that lawyer said that legally I am not entitled to anything, but for the sake of his future wife he will give me a fifty.

I am asking you now, was it worth while? My enemies should have business with lawyers!

23

Joe Meets a Book Agent

Poor Joe Katzman, the Carol Gonefsky Café and Restaurant and sometimes *Kibitzarnie* waiter. Each time I see him lately he has another story to make me listen about "What happened to him and because of Bercovich."

This story I won't forget and I must tell it to you:

It was at the mass meeting, at the Alliance Hall, that Joe again met Bercovich the *shadchen*. When Joe dropped a coin in the collection plate, Bercovich suddenly came up to him and said:

"Drop in a quarter for me, for I haven't any change with me."

So the movement cost Joe another twenty-five cents.

When the meeting was over and Joe started to go home, Bercovich walked along with him.

"Not so fast," Bercovich said. "What's your hurry? It is

your night off, anyhow. Walk slow. I have something to tell you."

"A *shidduch?*" Joe asked, feeling as if he has tasted some strong vinegar.

"Look, what a face he is making!" Bercovich said. "A *shidduch?* Sure, a *shidduch,* for what other business has a *shadchen* than to bring together nice young people and show them the way to a happy family life? A *shidduch,* you bet! Did you think I wanted to sell you a lot in Mudville, or shares in the new cemetery company?"

Joe was looking for a way to get rid of Bercovich, but the *shadchen* held him by his coat sleeve and kept on talking:

"I have for you a *shidduch* A-number-one, a *shidduch* from *Shidduchland.* The girl is a socialist and a radical— everything! A girl of the latest style. She is of a well-to-do-family, too—very rich people—but she wants a man that would love her just for herself, one that would not put down a figure how much he wants with her. Wait a minute, Joe. She is here, at this meeting. There, she is coming over."

The fact is that she was not coming over, but Bercovich got a hold of Joe's right arm and pulled him over to the aisle where he saw that girl walking toward the door. Outside, he introduced them saying,

"Miss Raskin, let me introduce to you Mister Joe Katzman. He is the party I spoke to you about, yesterday."

They shook hands.

"Is it the widower with the two children," she asked, "or is it the man whose wife eloped with a boarder?"

"No, no, no!" The *shadchen* was impatient. "It is Joe, the well-known waiter of the Gonefsky Café and Restaurant. Everyone in town knows Joe, the waiter."

"Excuse me," the girl apologized. "I had them mixed up."

The girl was not bad-looking and she had nice manners, but there was some mystery about her. It seemed to Joe maybe she had already been married before.

Bercovich made some excuse and left them in the street. So now it was Joe's duty, as a gentleman, to take her home.

They did not have far to walk, Miss Raskin living in the neighborhood, only four blocks from the Alliance Hall. When Joe said good-by she invited him to call on her. She lived with her parents.

It was hard for Joe to refuse, so he promised, and made the appointment for two days later, and, a waiter always being prompt, he called at the exact time. Miss Raskin gave Joe a cordial reception and she introduced him to her mother, a nice old lady, who wore a wig. Mr. Raskin was away in his custom tailor shop, on East Broadway.

Miss Raskin served tea and while they were talking a man called. He was a book agent who was selling sets of the "World's Greatest Gems of Literature" at one dollar cash and one dollar a month to pay until you get tired paying.

The caller wanted Miss Raskin to subscribe for a set of the books.

"But how do you know you can trust me?" Miss Raskin asked smilingly.

"It is all right about that," the book agent said; "I know your credit is good. I know all about your family. Your father has got a good trade in his store, and you have an uncle in Philadelphia who is worth between five and six hundred thousand dollars and he has no children. You have another uncle in Georgia who is a millionaire. You have two cousins in Boston that are very wealthy and charitable. Then when your old grandfather in South Africa dies your father will inherit a million English pounds. See, I know everything about you. Will you sign the order for the books?"

"Come some other time, please," Miss Raskin said. "You see, I have company now."

"Maybe the gentleman will buy a set of the books?" He began to talk to Joe about the quality of the books, of their binding and the easy terms of payment.

Joe's head was so upset by the great wealth of Miss Raskin's family that he took the agent's order blank and signed it.

The book agent left and Joe accepted another cup of tea, then a third and a fourth. By that time Joe was already half an hour late for work.

Of course, it was all on account of that book agent.

He left, promising to call again in a few days.

All day Joe was trying to memorize what the book agent told Miss Raskin in his presence:

"You have an uncle in Philadelphia who is worth between five and six hundred thousand dollars, and he has no children. You have another uncle in Georgia who is a millionaire." Then the two cousins in Boston and the old grandfather in South Africa. Can he live forever?

Next day comes Bercovich and urges Joe to hurry up and settle the *shidduch*. There are twenty or thirty other parties who want to marry Miss Raskin. So the poor waiter treats the *shadchen* to a good dinner, and Bercovich wishes Joe lots of *mazel* as he left.

Two days later and Joe was thinking of making another appointment with Miss Raskin, when something unexpected happened.

Bunimovitz, the landlord, who has a big tenement house in the neighborhood, comes to Gonefsky's with Gogelich, the banker. They sat down at a table and ordered some tea and cigars. Joe understood that they came to talk over a loan, hearing from others that Bunimovitz is in need of cash.

From the bits of their conversation that Joe caught it was understood that Gogelich would give only half the amount that Bunimovitz wanted to borrow.

Then—who was coming in? It was the same book agent that Joe met in Miss Raskin's house! He nodded to the waiter, then he went up straight to the table where Bunimovitz, the real estater, and Gogelich, the banker, are sitting. It was the nearest table to the counter where Carol is standing, taking cash for the cash register.

Every time Joe comes near the table the book agent lowers his voice. He was talking to Bunimovitz, and Gogelich was listening attentively.

Then the book agent left, and Joe could notice that Gogelich and Bunimovitz at last came to an agreement.

And then they left, too.

"Carol, please," Joe asked the owner of the restaurant, "did you hear what that book agent was talking to them? It is very important for me to know."

"Of what importance could it be to you?" Carol asked. "He did not speak of you at all. He first offered Mr. Bunimovitz a set of books on credit; then when Mr. Bunimovitz jokingly asked the agent how he knows that his credit was good, the agent started to tell that he knew Bunimovitz has one uncle in Philadelphia and another uncle in Georgia who are millionaires. He also said that he knew Bunimovitz has two cousins in Boston who are very rich and charitable, and that besides all that Bunimovitz expects a big legacy from a grandfather in South Africa."

"Enough, enough, Mrs. Gonefsky." That's all Joe wanted to know, and he went to tend to his customers.

You think that this was the end? No, sir; wait, there is a dessert coming.

This morning, when Joe came to work, Carol told him that a big box with books came for him by express and that she signed a receipt for him. When he opened the box and looked at the books, it was a set of the "World's Greatest Gems of Literature."

Joe got so mad that he telephoned the publisher to take back the books. Not a penny would he pay. But the answer comes that they are going to make Joe stick to the contract and that they have no worry about the payment, as the agent told them that he has an uncle in Philadelphia who is worth over half a million dollars, another wealthy uncle in Georgia, some very rich cousins in Boston, and so on and so on.

"You are laughing, eh?" Joe asked as he finished the story. "To you it is a joke, but how would you feel if you had been stung. Maybe you want to buy the set of books?"

24

Rain Water Is Good for the Complexion

Once I met Mr. Malkinson, the dry goods and notion jobber of Walker Street, and he asked me if I could get a doctor or maybe a lawyer for his daughter Sadele. "Ten thousand cash," he says to me, "no promissory notes, but a certified check or cash on the day of the wedding, and she is a brilliant girl besides. My Sadele is beautiful; no one will argue that. And she plays the piano and can dance like an expert. Didn't she win all the prizes in Tannersville last summer at the barn dances?"

"Lawyers and doctors I have by the bushel," I proudly informed Mr. Malkinson. "Let me take a look around and you'll hear from me. Have I an exclusive on your daughter or are you going to pass her out to all the *shadchens?*"

"Thirty-day exclusive," was the answer and we shook hands and parted.

Next evening I brought over to Malkinson's house a young physician from the Bronx, who was getting up a nice practice and also owned an automobile. We came to Malkinson's in his machine.

The father, the mother and the girl herself liked the young docor at the very start, for he was handsome, well built and dignified, just the kind of a doctor that success in life is almost sure. To tell the truth, from my point of view I wouldn't advise any young man who is less than six feet in height to study medicine. Now as I said, the doctor was well liked by the Malkinson family. But to my great surprise, Sadele Malkinson failed to please the doctor.

"So what's the matter!" I asked him when we were outside, after leaving the house.

"She is so unnatural," he said in disgust, "she uses so much *shmeer* on her face, she must be a member of the painter's union. A little help to nature is all right, but, Mr. Shulem, did you ever see such paint on a face? I'll never marry a girl who uses make-up!"

"Then you will remain a bachelor all your life," I told him. "If you want a woman that does not paint, then go to the Home for the Aged and you may find one, but I am not even sure of the ladies there."

"Then it is settled," the doctor said sternly. "I don't care to meet Miss Malkinson again."

So what could I do but report to Mr. Malkinson on the next day that the *shidduch* was off? I could not bring myself to tell him the real reason, for that would cause a family *shtuss,* as both the father and mother would insist that the girl should give up fixing her face.

Mr. Malkinson was unhappy. "What a loss! Such a fine young man," he said. "My daughter is almost in love with him."

148

Next day, Mr. Malkinson calls me up on the telephone and says:

"Mr. Shulem! My daughter is crazy for that doctor. I am willing to go to twenty thousand. Please go to see him again."

So I went to see the doctor again. When he heard of the second offer he began to soften.

"Well, I'll see her again," he said. "Maybe tonight she will not have so much paint on her face as last time."

We went there again in his machine. When we came I thought he would drop everything and run away, for on that night Miss Malkinson had on even more paint than at the first meeting. To me it seemed she made such an effort to look special, but to the poor young doctor she looked like an Indian in war paint.

Yet twenty thousand in real money is the best *shadchen*, and if the young doctor didn't fall in love with the girl at first sight, he did it at second sight. His manner changed entirely, but I noticed that all the time while he was talking to her he tried not to look at her face.

"Look here," I said to him when I got the opportunity to talk to him alone in a corner. "Don't be afraid of a little make-up. After you marry you will surely be able to persuade her to give up the habit. She is a lovely girl, after all. May I, you, and all our good friends have her weight in gold!"

Again I refreshed the doctor's memory about the *nadan* and he grew less uneasy as the evening passed. While everybody was enjoying themselves the doctor was called on the telephone from his office to go and see a patient.

"Duty before pleasure," he said, getting ready to leave, "especially a doctor's duty. I shall be back as soon as I can."

"Oh, I'm sorry," Sadele said sweetly, "and I envy you, doctor. It is so nice to speed to patients, knowing that you can give them relief. I wish I could go along."

"Come on!" he dared her, and the dare was accepted, amid the hearty laughter of the whole family.

The young couple left, and I remained to discuss details with Mr. Malkinson. He suggested after a while a little chess, because we had no difficulty as far as my fee was concerned. We were so absorbed in our game that we did not notice the hour until Mrs. Malkinson entered the room, frowning.

"I hope nothing happened to them," she said. "It is already two hours since they went away."

"Maybe they eloped and got married," Mr. Malkinson said with a big smile on his face. "Nothing better could happen. I'll add the cost of the wedding to the *nadan*."

"You," she said with a worried look on her face. "Always the joker. Look at the storm outside. Such terrible rain. They'll get drenched."

"I refuse to worry," said Mr. Malkinson. "I was worried when Mr. Shulem told me the *shidduch* was off, but not now! And furthermore, my dear wife, Sadele is no baby."

Just at that moment we hear an automobile stop in front of the house.

"They are here! They are here!" And Mrs. Malkinson raced toward the door to meet them.

They were both wet from the rain. I looked at the girl's face—all the paint had been washed off.

"She is beautiful, she is charming; she is the sweetest girl I ever met," the doctor whispered in my ear. "Now I see it; now I see it!"

"Yes," I remarked, "I've heard it said before that rain water is good for the complexion."

25

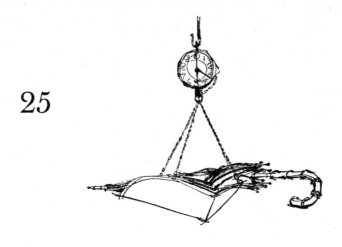

A Wife for a Widower

And they say women are fickle!

Solomon was a wise king, and when he said that it is better to go to the house of the mourning than to the house of feasting he hit it on the nose. As a *shadchen* I almost always prefer to go to funerals than to weddings, for purely business reasons.

Let me tell you why.

People believe that every wedding brings new business for the *shadchen*. This is assuming that the example set by the wedded couple will be followed by many others of the marriageable young men and girls who are present at the wedding. In fact there is nothing so discouraging to matrimony as a wedding. I am sure you have heard the jokes cracked by the friends and the *machutonim* at the expense of the bride and bridegroom, while they are still standing under the *chupah*. The usual comments go something like this:

"He didn't get the full $10,000, did he?"

"No. He got $4,000 in cash, and for the rest he got notes which her daddy will never pay."

"He looks scared."

"You bet your sweet life he does. But nothing can help him now."

"Poor Samuel! Now he's a married man."

That is what you hear at a wedding, but how different the talk is at a funeral!

"He was such a devoted husband."

"She was such a great help to him."

"They lived so happily, and nothing but death could part them."

Such remarks are more effective and bring better results for the *shadchen* than the most silver-tongued arguments. Is it any wonder that I, a *shadchen*, like to go to funerals?

It was Weiss, the undertaker, who once tipped me off that Mr. Farfel, a man of thirty-five and in good circumstances, had lost his beloved wife. Here, of course, was a business opportunity. So I went to the funeral.

"She was a remarkable woman," I heard some one of the friends say, "and she loved him as no woman ever loved a man. Last summer she made him go to the country, while she remained in the city to take care of his business. In every letter she asked him to forget the business and the family and just have a good time. And whenever she learned that a pretty girl was to leave New York on her vacation, Mrs. Farfel urged her to go to the same hotel where her husband was stopping. She was one in a million."

All this sounded very unnatural to me. I could see where a wife would send a husband away on a vacation, but to have pretty girls look her husband up at a hotel? This I never heard of!

So, I began to inquire. Weiss supplied a little information, but it was Bercovich, another *shadchen*, who gave me the real facts. And Bercovich had no reason to be angry because he had been paid his fee in full.

Emmis Farfel was the son of a very trusting father. Bercovich made the *shidduch* between Emmis and Ida. Emmis was promised a sum of money, with which he planned to enlarge his store. He never got the money from his *machuton*. Emmis was like his father, he believed and trusted everyone. So, the wedding took place and the father-in-law kept putting him off, and when the baby was born it was too late to look for the *nadan*.

A change came over Emmis Farfel when the baby came. He no longer trusted anybody. He also began to pester his wife, Ida, to ask her father for the *nadan* he was promised. The poor woman was embarrassed, so she tried to make it up to Emmis by being nice, such as his taking a vacation alone, and it was all right for him to look at pretty girls, and so forth.

During the week of mourning, I visited Mr. Farfel in his house, offering him the customary consolation. I saw that he was very much disconsolate, but I know from experience that the more a widow or a widower mourns, the more grief they show—the sooner they marry again.

And would I have any competition from Bercovich? I doubted it, because he had failed Mr. Farfel once.

After four weeks had passed I felt that it was not out of place to talk to Mr. Farfel about getting a mother for his daughter of seven.

"My little girl is with my mother," he said. "And about myself I must do as my wife requested."

Then he told me that his wife left a will, asking him to

marry a young widow who was a frequent caller at their house.

The will read:

> Should I die, I would like my husband to marry Mrs. Ganz. I know he likes her. She is a very lively woman and would make him happy.

"Do you really like her?" I asked him.

"Not to such extent as to be in love with her," Mr. Farfel answered. "But I guess I'll have to comply with my wife's last wish. The dear angel, may she rest in peace!"

"Do you want me to act as *shadchen* between you and Mrs. Ganz?" I asked.

"Not so soon," he answered. "Why the hurry? Let us wait another two weeks."

Two weeks after that last talk I called on Mr. Farfel, in his artificial-flower store.

"*Nu?*" I asked. "Shall I start?"

"No," he answered, looking as if he had just awoke from a nightmare. "Yesterday I discovered another will. Here it is. Read it."

This was his wife's second will:

> As I expect to die in the near future, I would like to advise my dear husband to marry Miss Glikson. He used to admire her blond, wavy hair, and at a wedding he enjoyed dancing with her.

"What are you going to do now?" I asked. "Do you like this girl better than the widow?"

"I do," he answered; "but the question is, Which of the two wills is the last one? My wife, the dear soul, neglected to date them."

"Then you have a right to make your choice," I suggested. "Shall I go and talk to Miss Glikson?"

"Let us wait another week or two," he begged me. "This is a very serious matter. I have to think it over carefully."

So I made up my mind to let him alone for another two weeks, but before that time expired he came to me.

"What caused you to make this long trip from the Bronx?" I asked.

"I decided in favor of Miss Glikson," he said. "And, to be frank with you, I do not want Miss Glikson so much as I do not want the widow. Mrs. Ganz is a charming woman, but she already has had three husbands."

"All right," I said. "Tomorrow I shall go and talk to her."

But the girl was not home when I called. Her mother told me that she had gone away to the country on her vacation.

When I returned home, Minnie, my wife, informed me that Mr. Farfel had called me up on the telephone. He had very important news for me.

Without removing my hat or coat or putting down my brief case I went to Mr. Farfel's store, in Wooster Street.

"What is the good news?" I asked him.

"Did you speak to Miss Glikson?" he asked.

"Not yet," I answered. "She is on her vacation in Tannersville."

"Good!" he exclaimed. "It is very fortunate that you did not speak to her, for I have found three more wills. Look at them!"

I took the three scraps of paper which he handed me and read them.

In one, she of blessed memory asked her husband to marry a Miss Fried, reminding him that he once took her out rowing and had made remarks about her beautiful figure. In another she asked him to marry a Mrs. Fein-stein, who had divorced an aged husband and was drawing alimony. In the third will, which, in fact was the fifth, she advised him to marry a Miss Guterman, a schoolteacher, saying:

> I know that my husband had a fancy for her. Once while we were at an outing he took six snapshots of her with his camera.

"What are you going to do now?" I asked. "None of the wills was dated, so how are you going to decide which will to obey?"

But Mr. Farfel did not hear me. He was very deep in thought. Evidently he was thinking of the happy bygone days.

"Such a darling woman," he mused to himself. "Always ready to sacrifice her own happiness for mine. She always felt that her father was dishonest to me in not giving me the *nadan* as promised. She spent her life in trying to be good to me. She always thought she was not good enough for me. But—such a darling wife."

I wanted to say something, but he interrupted me by a sudden resolve which came to him like an inspiration:

"I am not going to marry any of them, for none of them can take the place of my darling wife. I shall remain true to her memory until my last day."

He folded the five wills together and put them away in a drawer and I went home and told all of it to Minnie.

"There are fickle men in this world," she remarked.

26

Efficiency

The first time I heard mention of efficiency was at a lecture given by Mr. Plaudersak, the lecturer, who told his audience how a certain professor came to the idea of saving energy and doing more work. The professor was watching bricklayers at work on a new building, and he noticed that in laying the bricks they were making a lot of unnecessary movements with their hands—and at regular union rates. So the professor worked out a system by which every movement of the hand turned out real work. A Brownsville builder who happened to be at the lecture remarked that the only way to make a man do an honest day's work is to pay him by the piece—that is, by the number of bricks he lays.

I have a story about Mendel Rivkin, the raincoat manufacturer, and this efficiency theory. It was a very good story, so let me write it down.

You know Rivkin's son Isidor. So of course, you know that he is a college graduate and a *shlemiel* that is not fit for anything practical in life. He is always thinking up great schemes for making millions, but never making a single cash dollar. And seeing that he needs a start in real business, his father took him in his factory to learn the business. Now, do you think he learned anything? Instead of learning he began to teach the father—yes, teach him efficiency.

He started with the men who sew on the buttons on the coats. He showed him that much time is wasted if the same man is pulling the thread through the needle and sewing on the button. He divided the work in three. One man to cut up pieces of thread, each piece just enough for one button, and to prevent waste of material. Another to pull the thread through the needle. And the third to sew on the button. So his father tried it for one day. Efficiency? Izzy's efficiency the competitors should only have.

So Izzy begins to investigate why his system is not working and he discovers that the man who was pulling the thread through the needle had a pair of arms that were too long for the purpose, and Izzy thinks that maybe shorter arms would accomplish more. So he puts a girl in a man's place and attached a machine called a pedometer to her arm. The results are even worse than the day before.

So Rivkin said to him: "Look here, Izzy; I have been conducting my business without efficiency for thirty years, and, thank God, I have a big business and real estate property, and I am rated twice as much as Sigmund Pompushke, who wanted to get you for his daughter. You attend just to business and leave efficiency alone.

"Better still," continued Izzy's father, "get married and become efficient with your father-in-law's business. Tell me, how come didn't you marry Selma Pompushke? A nice girl she is, though her father I don't like, so tell me, why not?"

"Papa I'll tell you," Izzy confided slowly. "Selma is a nice girl, but after four years of college training, you just don't take a chance. Everything has a basis. I can prove by the slide rule that my new efficiency ideas not only will save time and material for you, but more important, I can keep your employees happier, give them less operations to do with better movements. They will be sixty per cent less tired after an eight-hour day, and when they go home from work they can enjoy their family. . . ."

"Wait, wait a minute, my expert," interrupted Mendel Rivkin, "I don't give a continental if the help enjoys their family, or if they are tired or how much motion they save. All I want is production, and without college efficiency. What about Selma?"

"But Papa!" said Izzy, "you don't understand modern thinking, you are old-fashioned."

"So, I'm new-fashioned when I send you to college," echoed the father. "I think I'll be sorry about that college for a long, long time. Izzy, I still think you ought to marry Selma and go in her father's business with efficiency, and in six months I'll have no competition."

"I have to disagree with you," said the son, cleaning his glasses with a special treated paper. "Papa, there is even efficient paper today to scientifically clean glasses. With this paper the lenses remain free of *shmutz* thirty per cent longer."

"Bah!" was the father's answer and he walked away in disgust.

The argument continued after Mendel and his son left the factory to go home and all Mr. Rivkin could hope for was for his son to get married and make a *mishmosh* out of somebody else's business.

While eating, Izzy started up again with, "You know today there is machinery that can pick a wife for a man and tell you what horse will win a horse race?"

"What kind of talk is that, Izzy; horses and wives," said the father, "how can you mix animals with a wife? Maybe Selma don't want you. If she'll take you today, I'll give the nadan. I'll make it up in six months' time."

Just then I rang the doorbell and Mrs. Rivkin opened up to let me in. I put down my brief case and umbrella, said a "hello" to everybody and Mr. Rivkin was glad to see me.

"Sit down, Mr. Shulem, here's a cigar," said the father of Izzy. "I hope you have something for my college boy, my Mr. Efficiency. Marry him off for me or you'll have to call Weiss the undertaker to take me away."

"It's not that at all, Mr. Rivkin," I said, "your Izzy and I have had a lot of talking lately. He's making an expert out of me, an efficiency expert."

"Oy! Oy!" moaned Mr. Rivkin. "Shulem, you're in for trouble. Go out of business before you go bankrupt!"

"How can I go bankrupt?" I said. "Stock I don't carry, creditors I have none, so tell me how can I go bankrupt?"

"All right, so don't go bankrupt," said the annoyed father, "tell me what brings you here?"

"To see Izzy," I said. "Izzy, you are right, efficiency can be good for a *shadchen*. Rivkin, you got to be up with the times to make a success today. And your Izzy is both. He teaches me new tricks every time I see him. And they work. Now take Selma . . ."

"Shulem, you—you take Selma and her father in the bargain," stammered Mendel Rivkin.

"No, my old-fashioned friend," I said. "Izzy is again right. Because of today's efficiency experts, not only can the bricklayer build a house faster and a button sewer sew a button quicker, but by a scientific efficiency study, I, Morris Shulem the *shadchen,* have been able to make changes in Selma."

"Did you really, Mr. Shulem?" Izzy asked.

"Yes, my boy, only because of the new methods," I said. "Selma, now has smaller eyebrows, her hips are, *eppis,* I don't know, maybe a half a foot smaller. She is changed all over. Everything is now efficiently ready for you to take over, Izzy; everything, except one thing."

"*Nu,* Shulem," asked Mr. Rivkin, "What's the one thing?"

"Do you remember when I first brought Izzy and Selma together," I said. "Mr. Pompushke offered $10,000 *nadan.* Today he won't part with one cent. . . . "

"Then he can't have my Izzy," said Mr. Rivkin indignantly.

"What's the matter, a few minutes ago you were pushing Izzy to your competitor," I said.

"Competition is one thing. When it's mixed up with efficiency for the competition, it's O.K.," said Rivkin, "but for me to stand four years of college expense and six months of trial efficiency mistakes in my factory, that Pompushke is asking and taking for granted too much! Not on your tin type!"

"Wait, Papa," injected Izzy. "Mr. Shulem, did Selma make those changes like the book quoted?"

"Yes, the changes are there," I said happily, "and Mr. Rivkin, I understand the young couple plan to be married in three weeks from Sunday, and at Izzy's suggestion I am leaving my bill."

"What bill?" shouted the elder Rivkin.

"Here, read it," I said handing Rivkin a printed invoice, marked No. 1. "Izzy even made me efficient. Now I have invoices."

I thought Mr. Rivkin would break his neck, it got so red when he looked at my invoice which read:

Mr. Mendel Rivkin
New York City, N. Y.
  For efficiently matching Selma Pompushke
  and Izzy Rivkin $1,000.00
            PAYABLE ON PRESENTATION

"Incidentally, Mr. Rivkin," I concluded, "Mr. Pompushke is expecting to see your deposit of $10,000 in the bank for the couple."

I think Rivkin almost had a stroke by the time I left, but by the end of the week the *machutonim* were discussing a merger of business as well as families.

27

Why Girls Spend Their Money on Clothes

Benchy, my grandson, was reading to me from an English paper about the shopgirls who spend all their money on dresses.

"Let me tell you, the girls are right," I said to Benchy.

If a woman comes to me with a daughter who has five or six hundred dollars in the bank, and she wants me to obtain a nice young man for her, I say to her this: "Tell your daughter to take her money out from the bank, and dress herself up in the best that the money can buy. With $500 in cash she can get a widower with five children, but with nice dresses, a fur coat, and a little make-up she can capture the best catch in town.

Once there was a time when men were afraid to marry girls who dressed too swell, thinking they will continue doing so even after they are married. They were right. But things have changed and nowadays the young men don't think so anymore. In fact, it looks to me, they have stopped thinking altogether, they just fall in love with a yard and a quarter of silk, half a can of powder and a pair of fancy stockings.

Take it, dear readers, from me; Shulem the *shadchen* knows wherefrom he speaks. I say to every girl who intends to get a husband, "Dress well," and I say to every married woman who wants to keep her husband happy, "Keep on dressing."

Once I had a neighbor who lived next door to me, Zipkin was his name. He and his wife used to quarrel so often the whole block knew them. But a stranger could never tell they were quarreling, for they used a code of their own. For instance, she wanted to tell him she hates him like poison she says: "Sweetheart, I love you like honey cakes." And whenever he called her "angel" or "sugar plum" it meant witch. It is only by the voices one could tell they were quarreling—never from the words. Many times I interfered, trying to make peace, but I was not successful, so at last I advised them to separate.

They both agreed to begin divorce proceedings, and they made an appointment with a lawyer to meet at his office. Before going to the lawyer, Mrs. Zipkin dressed up in her best, not forgetting to fix up her face. She looked like a new woman. And when she came in my house with an excuse of borrowing a few pins from Minnie she says to me:

"Well, I have to dress well now and try to look attractive, for pretty soon, Mr. Morris Shulem, I'll be asking you to find me a new husband."

Mr. Zipkin was not at home at that time. He was to meet her outside of his lawyer's office, downtown. There she came at the exact hour, but as soon as Mr. Zipkin saw his wife his manner changed. "I think we have plenty of time yet," he said. "Let us go in a restaurant and have a bite. We'll see the lawyer later."

The woman agreed to take another lunch with her hubby. They had a friendly *shmoos* at the table, and after their meal was over, Mr. Zipkin proposed a visit to a nearby moving-picture theater. When they came out it was already too late to see the lawyer, and they began to talk of other things.

"Why are you not always dressed like that?" Mr. Zipkin pleaded with her. "I think I could never cease loving you if you would always look like today."

"I shall try to please you," Mrs. Zipkin promised.

Since then the couple never talked of divorce again. They still use the same language between themselves, but the words are spoken in a different tone. And when Mrs. Zipkin calls her hubby "honey cake," she means to say he is sweet.

Now, do you need better proof than that?

A college education is a good thing for a girl, but her dressmaker, not the professor, is the real accomplice of the *shadchen*.

Here, I'll give you a for instance:

Leah and Florence Feinberg, sisters, lived with their mother, a widow. Leah was a college graduate and the older of the two girls and was always busy with books and with settlement work. She worked as the manager of the Center Settlement House Girls' Club. Here Leah met and made the acquaintance of big professors and some highbrows from uptown but mostly married men. But Florence was quite different from her sister; she did not go to college, she went from high school to work, for she liked to dress well; she went to dances and never let a chance for a good time go by.

Of course, Leah didn't like her younger sister's behavior, and often she lectured her and begged her to give up over-dressing and going to dances and go to night-school college. But Florence would say: "I'm a young girl and I want to have some fun."

The mother had something to say, too. "If you would take Florence to your settlement," she would say to Leah, "she would surely change and be like you. Honestly, the best thing that can happen is for me to see a *shadchen* and get you both settled."

But Leah wouldn't even hear of taking her sister to the Center Settlement House and as for a *shadchen*, that was out of the question. "The idea!" she'd say. "Bring a girl like that, with short skirts and a face full of powder, among those highly cultured people. What would they think of me!"

The mother begged her again and again. And when Florence promised to do her hair in the manner her sister desired and dress a little more quietly, she took her along. All the way to the Center Settlement House, Leah kept lecturing her sister how to keep herself, not to be con-spicuous and so on.

There was a dance that night at the Centre Settlement House, and of course Florence danced. People noticed her, especially the assistant head worker, and to Leah he said:

"Did that beautiful girl come with you? She is a won-derful dancer. Who is she?"

"My sister," Leah answered, blushing. I guess she didn't like it at all that the assistant head worker was noticing so much of her younger sister.

"Please, will you introduce me to her?" he begged Leah.

"She is not a college girl, Dr. Wolf," Leah said. "You mustn't expect to find her talk interesting."

It seemed that the assistant head worker was not the only one charmed by Florence. Everybody thought she was wonderful, and the head worker himself, Dr. Paulney, said to Leah: "We never knew you had such a charming sister. Why didn't you bring her here before?"

Florence was asked to come often, but next time when Leah went with her sister, Leah herself dressed like Florence. The assistant head worker married the younger sister and Leah learned the hard way, "that clothes make the woman," and is now engaged.

Up-to-date clothes could put all *shadchens* out of business!

28

The Phantom Bridegroom

One day—it was on a Monday—while I was resting in my office, at home, there comes a visit from a young man, who said he was from Mudville, N. Y., and he asks me to help him out in an important matter. He was to get married on the next day to a young girl of his town, but there was no one to perform the wedding ceremony. So he wanted me to get him a rabbi to officiate and also a few nice people to participate in the feast.

"I am well-to-do," the visitor, whose name was Mr. Zhulik, said, "but I have no relatives in my town. Please, I would like to ask you to invite five or six decent couples to be my guests at the wedding. I will pay their fare both ways, and remunerate you for your trouble."

"It is no trouble at all," I assured him, "but who was your *shadchen*, may I ask you?"

"I had no *shadchen*," he explained. "The girl worked

in my store as bookkeeper and stenographer, and I fell in love with her."

I forgave him with a big laugh for leaving me out of the *shidduch*. He had come to me after all, I told him.

"There is one more thing I would like to ask of you," he added. "My bride's parents are poor, and I would like to save them the expense of the wedding supper. Now, if your wife would undertake to supply us with a nice table—you know, roast duck, salad, pies—all that goes with a nice wedding supper. And I would pay her liberally."

"First I must ask my wife," I said.

Minnie agreed to undertake the job of caterer, for she is an excellent cook and likes to cook. She commenced with the preparations for maybe twenty people.

"Now, what will all that cost?" the visitor asked, taking out a blank check from one pocket and a fountain pen from another.

Again I consulted Minnie. Her bill would be $40; railroad tickets for six couples, pots and baskets in which to carry the wedding banquet, and minor expenses amounting maybe to $25 more.

"That is sixty-five dollars," Mr. Zhulik said. "And now I will give you a fifty for your trouble. Will that be all right?"

"It is too much," I said excitedly.

"It is not too much at all," Mr. Zhulik said. "I am considering your wife's trouble. She will have to do a lot of cooking."

He wrote out his check and, as soon as he signed it, he angrily pounded the able with his fist, exclaiming:

"*Shlemiel!* What did I do? Instead of $115 I made it out for $215, and this my last blank check!"

I felt sorry for him, because of the excitement in getting married. Then I thought for a minute and said:

"I shall pay you out the additional hundred, but I have only sixty dollars in cash. I shall bring you the other forty tomorrow, when I come to your wedding."

"You will bring me only thirty," he said, "and ten dollars should your wife have for a new hat."

Minnie thanked him. Mr. Zhulik left the house, taking along my sixty dollars in cash.

"Don't forget," he said at the door. "The eight-fifteen in the morning. Please be on time."

After he had left, Minnie commenced her marketing. All day until late at night she was roasting, cooking and frying. She baked *kitkes* with raisins, peach pies and apple pies and sponge cake. She roasted ducks, cooked fricassee, fish, made salads and dessert. And, I tell you, everything so good that it was fit for a king.

While she was busy with the cooking, I went looking for my people. A rabbi to perform the ceremony I got and also four couples, who were only too glad to spend a day in the country—and as guests!

Next day our wedding party met at the station, a full hour before the train. We were to board from the station at 125th Street, as the rabbi lived in that section of the city.

Every one of us, except the rabbi, was carrying a basket or a bundle in which the wedding supper had been packed away.

Oh, yes, and Minnie, my wife, brought a new summer bonnet, which made her look ten years younger.

At last comes our train. The cars are almost filled with people who boarded at Grand Central, and we have to walk through from one car to another to find seats.

In one of the cars we came across a party of people dressed for a holiday and all carrying with them all sorts of packages, bundles and baskets.

"Another wedding party," one of them said as we entered the car.

We passed and went to another car. There we found seats and we made ourselves comfortable and we were all excited and happy.

At the next station more passengers boarded our train, and among them was another party of men and women also *shlepping* baskets and bundles. One basket was partly uncovered and from a corner a long twisted fresh-baked loaf stuck out. There was no doubt about it that these people, too, were going to some gay party.

Yet, to be sure, I asked one of them.

"Are you going to a wedding?"

"Yes," he replied. "And I suppose you, too, are going to one. And how far are you going?"

"Mudville," I said.

"Mudville!" he exclaimed, very much surprised. "I did not think there were to be two weddings in that village today. Is yours a rich wedding?"

"The bride is poor, but the bridegroom is wealthy," I said.

At that moment a man came in from the next car, and coming over straight to me, he inquired:

"May I ask you, *landsman,* are you going to a wedding?"

"Yes," I answered. "Here are two groups going to two weddings, and both of them take place in Mudville!"

"Funny," the inquirer remarked. "I am going there, too."

Then I commenced to suspect. The three of us looked at one another, but we were afraid to speak.

At last one of the men ventured to ask:

"So who is going to be married?"

"*Oy*," I said, "I am afraid nobody is going to be married."

And then everyone recited the same story of the visit of this mysterious Mr. Zhulik, his big check which was written on his last blank and the amount that he got in cash for it. One man paid him a full hundred.

There was such a *shtuss* in the car—such an excitement and commotion in our three wedding parties. We decided to get off at the next station and take a train home. We all had our return tickets—and bought by our own money.

We had to wait six hours for a train to take us back home, because in the excitement we go off at a local depot where the 8:15 in the morning stops to accommodate the hired help that goes to work in the suburbs.

Hungry we couldn't get because *essen* we had enough for an army. So for six hours we ate.

29

Love at an Undertaker's

One day, about a week ago, a man above middle age, poorly dressed and shabby, came into Gonefsky's Restaurant here and ordered a Danish and coffee, and then proceeded to ask Joe how much he made a week. That struck me funny, for I never saw the man before, and to ask a personal question of Joe, the waiter, interested me. So, instead of Joe answering his question, I asked him:

"Why do you want to know? Are you a *shadchen?*"

"If I were a *shadchen,*" he said, "I wouldn't have to worry about my daughters. I have six of them and all of marriageable age. They are nice-looking girls, speak a good English, play the piano and can dance, too, but I have no money to give them. And that is where the trouble comes in. If a girl can't be born with a bag of gold she should not be born at all. Young men who meet my daughters fall in love with them, but when they find out that their father is poor they run away."

"*Nebich*," I remarked.

"We have company at our house almost every night in the week," the man continued. "Whether they mean business or not, young men like to come to our house and be entertained by my daughters' singing and playing the piano, and by my wife's cooking. *Ach, mein Gott*, what she cooks for them! She spends fourteen hours in the kitchen every day baking *shtrudels*, lemon pies, honey *teiglech* and ginger cookies for our visitors. She also prepares for them all kinds of punches and lemonade.

"My daughters make friends easily. Every evening my wife and I are called out from the kitchen to be introduced to some new friend. Old friends vanish and new ones arrive. After the introduction we go back to the kitchen, so as not to be in the way of the young people."

The man took a bite of Danish and a sip of coffee and then continued:

"One evening a little girl, about nine or ten, comes to the house and asked for her father. She had been told by some one that he is in my house. So I went to the parlor and said: 'Excuse me, ladies and gentlemen. A little girl here is asking for her father.' Three young men jumped from their seats and leaped through the window to the fire escape. My daughters fainted. The other young men left in a hurry too. I still have the three hats and the over-coats that the three married men left in their hurry to get away."

"Are your daughters still entertaining?" I asked.

"More than ever," he said. "There are so many young men tonight that there is nothing left for me to eat. Every-thing goes down the throats of those *fressers*. So my wife told me to go out and eat in a restaurant."

I pitied him so much that I offered to buy him another cup of coffee and a sandwich. He seemed to be touched by my hospitality, and taking out a photograph from his pocket he showed it to me.

"This is my oldest daughter," he said. "Isn't she a fine girl? I wish she'd marry some good, honest man who earns a moderate living; he can even be a plain fellow."

"She is a very nice young lady," I said. And that wasn't mere flattery. Indeed, the girl looked beautiful.

"Her looks are nothing, comparing to her wisdom," the father said. "I wish you would meet her and talk with her."

I introduced myself to the gentleman and when I told him I was a *shadchen* he hoped I could help him. I told him that Joe Katzman, the waiter, who was serving us, is a fine young man with steady habits. I called Joe over and showed him the picture of the man's oldest daughter and told Joe of the many guests that come to the man's house.

The blood rushed to Joe's face and he began to stammer.

"I would like to, but I wouldn't feel comfortable to meet her in the presence of all the young men who come to your house," Joe finally said.

"But you can meet her at the office where she works, that is Weiss' undertaking establishment," the father said.

"Weiss?" Joe asked, much surprised. "Your daughter works for Weiss, the undertaker? For how long?"

"About eight years," he said.

Joe thought that the best time for him to see the girl was between nine and ten in the morning, before he goes to work, and before Weiss comes to his downtown office. Weiss has another office uptown, where he stays until noon.

Joe was a little superstitious, and every time he has to pass an undertaker, he would cross over and walk on the other side of the street. But he decided he would go and meet the young lady.

Joe was still nervous when he entered the office, but Miss Malkin—that was her name—put him at ease right away.

"You are Mr. Joe Katzman," she said. "Be seated, please." And she pointed to a chair near her desk.

As soon as Joe sat down the door opened and two men brought in a large, heavy coffin. Joe commenced to fidget. The very thought of a corpse scared him to death, and he was about to jump from his seat and run outside. But then, to his great surprise, he noticed Bercovich, the other *shadchen,* peeping through the window and grinning at him. Bercovich! At that moment he had only one wish—only should Bercovich drop dead and be brought in, in a coffin.

Joe could hardly hear what Miss Malkin was saying to him. He was trapped. Here he was afraid of the dead, inside, and of the living, outside.

"You should excuse me, just a minute," Miss Malkin said to him. "I have to go to the garage and give some orders to the men."

He was alone. Imagine how Joe felt. Afraid to turn his back to the coffin, yet the fear of meeting Bercovich in the street was even greater. And then all of a sudden he heard something like a screech. He jumped and ran for the door. He was too afraid to look, but to his great fortune a streetcar stopped right in front of Weiss' establishment and he jumped in just when it was ready to start.

Joe fell into the first available seat and closed his eyes, trying to forget all the terrors of the last ten minutes.

"Fare, please!"

It was the conductor, and Joe handed him a quarter.

"Take out for two!" Joe heard a familiar voice giving orders to the conductor, and looking up, he saw it was Bercovich the *shadchen.*

"Well, what do you want now?" Joe asked, wondering

where he got the courage to talk. "Why don't you mind your own business?"

"I do mind my business," Bercovich replied. "But that *shadchen* from Rivington Street is not a practical man. He does not follow through like I do. When I get a tip on a possibility I don't leave the possibility out of my sight. And you are my possibility. I even hire a partner for a possibility. That was one of my partners you met in Gonefsky's who posed as the father of the girl that you just met. He was sent to the café by me. Well, what do you say?"

"What do I say?" answered Joe. "Just two words. Drop dead!"

30

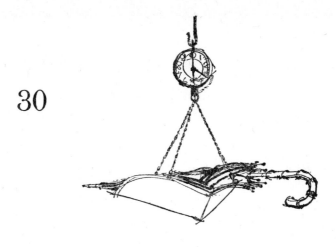

Free Advice

You can never guess what a girl is gong to be after she marries, from what she is before being married.

Young man, if you want to get married do not try to be too careful, or too wise. This is Shulem the *shadchen*'s advice. Never try to guess about a girl because what she is, she is.

Look at Simon Krulewitz. He wants to be practical, so when I offer him a lovely girl like Bella Mandelbaum, he refuses and marries a cook. He did not listen to his family, who thought it was below him to marry a servant. He said, "I want a wife that will keep house for me, cook a good meal, and not spend all her time at the beauty shop." Do you think his expectations were realized? Poor Simon! *Nebich*. He ought to have known better. After he married the cook, she would not even dip her finger in cold water. All the time she was busy getting new dresses, but never could she spare a few minutes to cook an egg for him. "I have done enough cooking in my life," she said, "and now I want to enjoy and have a good time."

So now, Simon Krulewitz is compelled to take her out every evening to restaurants for dinner. And that is what he got for being so practical.

Joe Malkinson was a struggling young lawyer, just starting out, and when I introduced him to Bella Mandelbaum —the same one that Krulewitz rejected in favor of the cook —he was a little shaky in his mind about her. He was afraid, he told me, that he would not be able to provide for her in the style she was used to. She was real fine, I tell you, and everything she wore was of the latest. His friends advised him against marrying her, saying, "What do you want a girl like that for? Your earnings will not be enough for her clothes alone, not counting the beauty parlor; and you will need a maid to keep house for her."

But Malkinson was so much in love with the girl that he married her in spite of his friends and his own fears, and now there is not a happier husband than Malkinson and there is not a better housekeeper than Bella. A complete change came over her after she married. Now she dresses plainly, curls her hair herself and stays home most of the time. She learned to cook and does all the housework. "I have spent enough of my time in idleness," she said to me when I called at the house not long ago. "Oh, Mr. Shulem, housework is pleasant and delightful! And my husband likes the dishes I cook for him; he licks each plate clean."

Could you ever expect such a turn?

Yes, that is what I said before, you can never guess what a girl is going to be after, from what she is before.

Barney Goldman is another newlywed, and I was his *shadchen*. Not long ago I met him in the street.

"Well, how is married life?" I asked.

"Don't ask," he answered, "the woman you gave me is a nag and a scold, a regular witch."

"You don't say!" I exclaimed, for I could hardly believe he was serious. "A nice, quiet, sweet soul like Sadie Kronberg should turn into a nag and a scold? Not to say a witch? Are you kidding, Mr. Goldman?"

"This is no time for kidding," he said. "I have told you the exact truth. What she was and what she is now are two different things."

"May I ask you a question?" I said. "Maybe you are giving her cause for scolding?"

"I am sure that my conduct toward her is perfect, A-number-one," he asserted. "She has no reason for nagging or scolding."

"Then I must go and see her," I volunteered. "Perhaps I will find out. Of course, she must not know that you spoke to me of her."

"If you want to see her," Mr. Goldman advised, "do it right now. It would be much better than when I am home."

I did as Mr. Goldman bid me, and when I came there I found Mrs. Goldman entertaining some of her women friends.

"Oh, it's Mr. Shulem!" she greeted me in a most cordial manner, taking both my hands in hers and dragging me to the parlor where the ladies were seated. "Ladies," she introduced me, "I want you to meet the man who gave me the greatest happiness in life. This is Mr. Shulem the *shadchen.*"

And then, leading me to a corner where a fine, shapely girl with shell-rimmed glasses was sitting, she addressed the girl.

"Bertha, you'd better get acquainted with Mr. Shulem. He is a reliable *shadchen,* the best one in the city, and I am sure he can suit you. All the couples who were married through Mr. Shulem are happy."

"Are you happy, Sadie?" the girl asked jokingly. "How do you find married life?"

"Only heaven should be so good," Mrs. Goldman asserted.

Just at that moment it came to my mind what her husband had said only a half an hour ago—"a witch."

So which could it be? I made up my mind to find out.

"It is so good to have a husband," Mrs. Goldman continued, addressing the girl with the glasses. "I am so happy with Barney; he is so good, so kind, and if you, Bertha, will get a husband like Barney, you will be happy also."

Well, I could hardly believe it was Mrs. Goldman who was speaking after what her Barney had told me. What could be his object in telling me that his wife was nagging and constantly picking at him?

"Pray," I said to Mrs. Goldman, "tell your friend more about your husband so I may get her, too, as a client."

Bertha laughed and the other ladies in the company joined her.

"I can say this," Mrs. Goldman readily replied, "that during the six months of our married life I never had an occasion to find fault with my husband. I found him better, kinder, and more lovable every day."

"I, as your *shadchen,* am very glad to hear that," I remarked, "but I wish, Mrs. Goldman, you would give me a written testimonial, as that would help me in my profession."

"That's right!" all the ladies in the room seconded my request, "and we shall all sign our names as witnesses."

It was a game to them, but I was quite serious. Mrs. Goldman drew up a testimonial which was to inform whoever may it concern that her husband, whom she married through Mr. Shulem the *shadchen,* is the best man living, only more so.

The other ladies signed their names as witnesses, and I took the paper and went home with it.

In about an hour comes Mr. Goldman to inquire.

"Well," he asked, smilingly, trying to hide his anxiety, "what have you found out?"

"Here, read it," I said, handing over his wife's testimonial.

He read it once and then over again. "How did you get it from her?" he asked.

"When I came there," I told him, "your wife was telling the ladies the sweetest things about you—that you are a model husband, the kindest man in the world. So I asked her to write it all down on paper and the other ladies to sign as witnesses."

"I can't understand it," Mr. Goldman was wondering.

"I can't either," I said, "but as a rule, all those women who like to pick on their husbands in private always boast of their husbands in public. Why they do it is a mystery to me, but human nature is full of mysteries."

Goldman was still staring at the testimonial.

"I shall let you keep this," I offered, "and whenever your wife commences her nagging, only produce her testimonial, written in her own handwriting, and she will stop— I am sure she will."

31

Benchy and the Papers

I have always been an easy fellow to get along with. I understand my own shortcomings as well as the next man's. Or almost as well. Being a *shadchen* is more than being a doctor, because I don't give pills; or even a lawyer, because I don't give advice. What I try to do is to understand a person and his needs and wants and bring that person to another person and help them understand each other. And it is just as simple as that. Believe me.

But, one thing that I can't stand is to have somebody wrinkle up my newspaper. Minnie leaves my paper alone until after I have looked at it. My girls haven't got the time in the morning to bother it. The only one I can't get to understand about my newspaper is my grandson Benchy. He not only turns the paper away from the folds, he mixes up the pages and always takes the surprises out of it for me. I could be resting or still asleep and Benchy will rush into my room and with a *gevalt* say:

"You know what? In the paper it says. . . ."

And that always spoils my day. Not so long ago Benchy gave me what he reads in the sports pages—a one-two punch! An acquaintance of mine was in the Sunday paper, and I want to tell you what Benchy read.

The story is actually about a client of mine. I stopped Benchy from reading it to me because I know the details. What actually happened was not in the newspaper, but, since Benchy woke me up, so I told him the correct story.

Some time ago I was visited by a middle-aged man, who said he came all the way from Kansas to get a wife in New York.

Naturally I questioned him about himself. I found out from him he was in business in a little town near Kansas City, Missouri, that he was in good circumstances and a widower.

"I have a good party for you," I said without looking in my book, "but first, you will have to prove that you are a widower before I introduce you to the lady. That is the way Shulem the *shadchen* always is conducting his business."

"All right," says he. "Suppose I bring you a picture photograph of myself standing and crying over my wife's grave? Will that do?"

"Splendid," I said. "Go ahead and bring me the picture, and meanwhile I'll make an appointment for you with a charming, lovely young widow and with no children."

Next day, my client from Kansas called with the photograph. It was just like he said. Here was a grave and a tombstone over it, and there he was standing and crying with his face in both hands, like a faithful husband should cry over his loving wife.

"This is fine," I said after seeing that picture of sincere grief and devotion.

So in the evening I took him by the widow. She made

a big spread on the table, as the custom is, and Mr. Rosenfeld cracked jokes and did tricks with his fingers for everybody's pleasure. He made a good impression on the young widow. By this time the match was as good as settled, I felt.

"You don't know what a devoted husband Mr. Rosenfeld was to his first wife," I said, holding up the picture to the young lady and her mother and her father who was with us just before we were ready to go. "Here you can see Mr. Rosenfeld standing over the grave of his wife, on the cemetery in Kansas, crying like few men ever cried. Just take a look, see how he is crying?"

The young widow looked at the picture and shouted: "Mr. Shulem! What does this mean? This snapshot was taken right here, in the city. This picture was staged by a photographer. I'm surprised at you!"

Mr. Rosenfeld got red like a turkey, and he began to explain. To prove he was a widower? That he can do positively. He only took the picture to save time. But he was told to take his hat and go.

So you see how a fool on earth can spoil a match that was made in heaven.

What was in the papers was that the lovely widow was suing Mr. Rosenfeld for false impersonation. Also hurt feelings.

That is one example, and here is another which, besides proving my ideas, has also a good moral for young men.

Not long ago I brought together a young manufacturer of ladies' cloaks with the daughter of Mr. Boginsky, the rich furrier. No, I can't tell you the full name of the young manufacturer, but for the sake of convenience we'll call him Max.

Bertha and Max met and liked each other from the start. Old Mr. Boginsky promised $20,000. I was to get the biggest sum I ever got as a *shadchen*'s fee. And every one who looked at the pair said they were created for each other. Such a fine match is seldom made, not even in heaven.

The engagement party was one of the most talked of affairs of the social life in Brooklyn. Even the papers printed notices. I was so proud I almost felt I was becoming too big for my skin. Everybody was happy, but then, *tzoris*.

Max had in his business a model, a girl who earned her livelihood by trying on coats that Max manufactured. Many times I called on Max and I found him to be on very friendly terms with the girl. But I thought this was only business, and that he was *kibitzing* her so she would remain plump and retain the exact form that is needed in that kind of business.

Then Benchy read to me a while back a story about a policeman who found a man's wallet with $1,200 in it and the policeman turned the money over to the captain in the station house.

"I wonder who lost the money?" I asked.

"There is nothing to identify the owner," Benchy said, "except a girl's picture that was found in the pocketbook, and on the picture it said: 'To Max, with love and kisses from Gertrude.'" The picture was printed in the newspaper.

I took a quick look at the picture and recognized the girl in a moment. It was the coat model that worked for Max.

What was I to do? I asked myself. Go tell Boginsky, or first go to Max and ask for an explanation? I could not make up my mind. I spent a whole day and an evening thinking.

I could hardly close my eyes all night. At last, with dawn, I decided to see Miss Gertrude, the coat model herself, and hear what she had to say about it. With my mind made up I fell asleep. In the morning, while my eyes were still heavy with sleep, I heard Benchy in my room. I also heard Minnie holler at him: "Leave your grandpa alone! He had a sleepless night."

"But there is something important for Grandpa to see," argued Benchy.

I jumped out of bed and yelled for Benchy to bring me the paper. It was as usual all wrinkled when he handed it to me.

"See, Grandpa, here is the picture of the man who lost the money. They found him out!"

And who was it? It was Max, the coat manufacturer.

I felt it was my duty to go to Boginsky's house, for in my opinion his family were the real sufferers because of this unfortunate affair. When I arrived there, a servant told me the whole family suddenly left for the Catskills. With a heavy heart, I went over to Max's cloak factory. He looked pale and nervous, and when he saw me, he made a rush toward his private office, but I caught up with him.

"Look here!" I said, as I squeezed myself in the half-shut door. "Don't shut me out. I didn't come to lecture you. Let bygones be bygones. You know it's all over with Miss Boginsky. Now, I have another proposition."

"*Nu*, so what is it?" he asked timidly.

"Marry that Miss Gertrude," I said. "You like her and she likes you, too; so, why not marry her and you'll both be happy? You don't need the money; you have plenty money of your own. A man of your business will be happier with a girl like your Miss Gertrude."

He gave me a look in my face to see if I was serious, and seeing that I was, he shook my hand, saying:

"Mr. Shulem, you are not only a great *shadchen*, but also a philosopher who knows his business to perfection."

They married, and I got my fee, but in justice to heaven, I must say that for this match nobody is responsible but Shulem.

32

Shulem Joins a Union

They say, in organization there is strength, but heaven help the *shadchen* who needs help from another *shadchen*. An honest *shadchen*, like an honest lawyer, has to work very hard to be a success in this practical world.

Take a look at Bercovich, my strongest competitor. Bercovich is such a liar, the likes of which you cannot find. If he says it is a day, it is neither day nor night, but a bag of clothes pins. And yet he is the most successful *shadchen* in New York. But an honest *shadchen* like me, Morris Shulem, has to wear out two pairs of shoes before he succeeds in having one match accomplished.

Once when I told Minnie, my wife, of my trip to Arverne and of the people I met there she remarked:

"You know, Morris, that $20,000 widow whom you met in Arverne, and Burik, the ladies'-sweater manufacturer, would make a fine match. It is about time that old *buchor* should settle himself. I cannot understand why you cannot marry him off."

"A good idea, Minnie!" I congratulated. "Just now I could not think of Burik. Telling the truth, I had given him up twice already. No girl seems to suit him, so maybe that widow will have a chance. Old bachelors yield easily to widows. I don't know why, but maybe is it that widows are more practical in the art of trapping a man than girls? You see, when a girl gets a fellow she has him broke before she marries him, but when a widow gets one, first she marries him and then she breaks him."

"True," Minnie agreed.

Next morning I left my house early, brief case and umbrella in hand, going straight to Burik's sweater factory, in Grand Street.

When I get within a block of the factory, I am stopped by a group of men who were walking on the sidewalk.

"Are you going to Burik's factory?" one of them asked me.

"Yes," I said, "but how did you guess it?"

"I can tell a strikebreaker by his looks," he answered roughly, "and you'd better go home, mister. We men from Burik's factory are on strike."

"But I am not a sweater maker," I argued. "I am a *shadchen*."

"Another guy just like you has given the same reason before," he replied, "and we are not going to let anyone fool us again."

There was nothing else for me to do but to go back. I walked around the block and tried to get in the factory through another entrance.

"Hey, you!" hollered at me a big fellow with a badge on his coat. "What do you want here?"

"I am a *shadchen* and I want to see Mr. Burik."

"You are one of them pickets," he said. "I saw you tal[k]ing to them, and if you don't move away quick I'll ha[ve] you arrested."

Just at the moment Mr. Burik happened to look throu[gh] the window. "He is all right," he called out to the spec[ial] officer. "Let him come in."

The special officer apologized and we shook han[ds]. Then I went up to Mr. Burik.

"This is my lucky day," he remarks as I entered his [pri]vate office. "You are the second *shadchen* to call on me [this] morning. Bercovich was here just about half an hour a[go]."

"And did he have something worth while?"

"Nothing new I would care for." Mr. Burik yaw[ns]. "Just girls that know how to spend money. Last wee[k he] offered me triplets. Three beautiful girls. They talk a[like] they dress alike and they look alike. I told him I w[ould] like to marry all three, but, ha! ha! who can marry t[hree] at one time? I would have to be a King Solomon to pic[k.] Shulem, you know what I did? I gave them a test, and [then] I would decide."

"Nu?" I wondered. "And what kind of a test di[d you] give the triplets?"

"I took each girl aside and asked her a question [that] would help me come to a decision."

"So what was the question?" My curiosity was g[etting] the better of me.

"I asked the first triplet how much two and two w[ere,] she said 'three,' and I thought she would be good t[o have] in the office when I have bills to pay. I asked the nex[t trip]let the same question and she said 'five' and then I t[hink] she would be good when it comes to collecting bill[s. But] when I asked the last one the question she said 'fou[r' and] she is the one to keep me honest."

"So which one did you take?"

"Not so fast, my friend Shulem, I'm still in the r̶.
None of the girls could fill out a size forty-two swe̶

"But I have for you a widow who is a regular mov̶
picture beauty and she has $20,000," I said.

"Is that all?" he asked.

"Why, you want more money?" I asked.

"You misunderstand me, Mr. Shulem," he explained. "I
did not ask you if that was all the money she had. What I
really wanted to know was whether she has other qualities
beside being pretty and having money."

"Old bachelors like you are no choosers," I snapped at
him, for I was really out of patience. "What more do you
want? You will be fortunate if she will want you. I have to
go and ask."

On my way out the pickets got a hold of me again, and
said that they would not let me go unless I join their
union.

"But I am not a sweater maker; I never worked in a
factory," I told them.

"Stop bluffing," the smallest fellow in the crowd yelled
at me. "We have heard the same story of the other strikebreaker, who also claimed to be a *shadchen,* but we made
him join the union just the same."

They surrounded me, took me up to an office where I
paid a dollar and fifty cents, and got my card as a member
of the Sweater Makers' Union, No. 45, of New York.

After I get my union card I am led to another part of
the office, and there I was handed a brand new crisp five-
dollar bill.

"What is that?" I ask.

"Strikers' benefit money," I am informed. "You'll get
that every week as long as the strike lasts."

It pays to be a union man, I said to myself.

Next day I made a trip to Arverne to have a talk with

the widow. After she listened to me for a while she became interested in my old bachelor Burik and she asked me:

"Can he speak French?"

"Why do you want him to speak French?" I asked.

"Well," she answered, "I made up my mind to marry only such a man who can speak French. If you can get me a nice gentleman who speaks French I'll marry him."

I looked over my notebook, but among the hundred and eighty-seven eligible young men that I had on my list there was not one who spoke French. So I decided to see Bercovich; maybe he has one.

"There is not a thing that I cannot get," Bercovich said when I came to him with a request to help me get a fellow who can speak French and who would be willing to marry a beautiful widow with $20,000. "I can get you fellows who speak French, Spanish, Italian, Turkish, and languages you never heard of."

It was agreed between us that as soon as Bercovich found the man, I was to arrange the meeting with the widow.

Two days later Bercovich telephoned me that he had found the man we wanted. I wrote to the widow, asking her for an appointment, and she answered me that she will come over to New York and meet the man in her father's home, which was a private house on the Concourse.

Bercovich is to bring the young man to the house himself, as he wanted to be sure of his seventy per cent of the *shadchen* fee which I promised him. The meeting was arranged for Thursday evening.

I came there early, ahead of Bercovich, and waited. He came promptly at the appointed time, and he brought the young man with him. He was tall and thin, looking as if maybe he has suffered from nervousness. The *nebich* would hardly open his mouth. When he was introduced to the widow, her parents, and to me, he merely shook hands with everybody and muttered something which no one could hear.

"He seems to be very bashful," Mr. Shifrin, the widow's father, said to me in a whisper and then he made a sign for all of us to go to the other room and leave the young man and his daughter to themselves, in the parlor.

There, in the next room, tea was served for us, but we had hardly touched the tea when the widow rushed into the room where we are sitting, and in an excited voice she cried to Bercovich:

"Take him away, you bluffer; he can't speak French, he can't even speak Yiddish!"

"*Shsha!* Calm yourself, Deborah," her father implored.

"I don't want him"—the young widow was raving mad; "he stutters terribly; I cannot make out one word what he says."

"I could not make out, either," Bercovich replied calmly. "You see, the way he spoke I thought it was French."

The party, which promised to be a gay one, broke up all of a sudden. The whole deal was designed by Bercovich to spoil my reputation.

I went home very sad, almost heartbroken, and there I found a card from the Sweater Makers' Union, Local No. 45, of Greater New York, asking me to report at the office of the union next morning at 7 A.M. sharp.

I reported promptly, and there, at the office, I was told that the strike was won and that I was to start work on the same day in Burik's factory.

You may think it is a joke, but I tell you I was almost sorry that I could not accept the job. Any workingman is much better off than a *shadchen*. At least he is part of an organization.

33

Married By Gossip

They say, where there is smoke there is fire, and the same is true with gossip. Only with a fire you need a fireman to put out the fire and with gossip a *shadchen* comes in handy.

One hears much these days of people getting married by using the telephone, telegraph, or wireless, but this is a story of a pair who were married by gossip.

One morning as Minnie is handing me my morning mail she says:

"Do you know, Morris, that there is a rumor on the block that Isidor Mirmelstein, that young lawyer, is courting Betsy Kanarik, the dressmaker?"

"No, I have not heard," I said, "but please leave me alone for just a few minutes to read my mail. Maybe there is something important which needs immediate attention. Business first and rumors next."

After my wife left I resumed reading my mail. That morning there were only two letters for me.

One was from a married woman who was soon to get a divorce; as she believed in preparedness, she wrote asking for an early appointment.

The other letter was typewritten, and it came from a widow who had a peculiar problem. Her husband smoked K——, a certain brand of cigarettes which gives coupons, the coupons being good in exchange for a cut-glass fern dish with artificial ferns. Recently the husband died, leaving only 994 coupons; so she wants me to find her a man who smokes the same brand of cigarettes, as she needs only 1,006 more coupons.

I presume this letter is the work of a joker—maybe even Bercovich—for people, as a rule, like to poke fun at the *shadchen*. And why? There is a simple reason. Those who are still unmarried are sore at him because he does not accommodate them, while people who are already married bear him a grudge for having already acommodated them.

"Well, Minnie," I said to her when she came back with my tea, "tell me about those rumors. Do you mean that pretty dressmaker who is supporting her widowed mother and two younger sisters?"

"Yes, that is the one," Minnie answered. "People in the block say that she and the lawyer are much in love with each other."

"I don't believe what people say," I argued. "I know better. Many times have I showed Lawyer Mirmelstein some good offers, but he said he is not yet ready to assume the responsibilities of a family. I offered him that wholesale grocer Altshuler's daughter with $5,000 and he refused. I offered him Ganz's daughter, the one who broke her engagement with Tamarkin, the dentist, and $7,000 cash in the bank, and he also turned me down. So how can you believe such nonsense that he will marry a poor girl with a family depending on her?"

"Well," my wife said, "you never can tell. Such rumors must have a foundation—and maybe you are losing a *shidduch?*"

Mirmelstein, the young lawyer, lives in our block, and there, on the ground floor where he lives with his parents, he also has his office.

In the afternoon I dropped in to see him, and I told him of the rumors that were floating around concerning him and Miss Kanarik.

"There is not a word of truth in it," he said. "Although the girl lives in the same house, I do not remember having spoken to her more than one neighbor would on passing another in the hall."

I was about to go, when Mirmelstein added:

"However, I am sorry for the girl, and I wish I could do something to offset the rumor. I'll go up tonight and ask her what I can do in this matter.

"You should do something," I implored. "As a *shadchen* I know how such rumors hurt a girl's chances."

"Well, I'll call on her tonight," he said, "and I will do everything to prove there is nothing in the rumor—absolutely nothing."

I went back home and I found Minnie busy preparing dinner.

"Well, what did Mirmelstein say?" she asked.

"That there is not a bit of truth in the rumor," I answered. "People like to brag about things which are untrue. It is all a lot of *shmoos,* but he is going to marry her as sure as daylight."

"If the rumors are not true, how is the thing going to happen?" Minnie was wondering.

"You just watch your Morris Shulem," I said.

Next day I paid Mr. Mirmelstein another visit.

"Yes, I saw her last night," he told me, "and am I mighty glad I did, for I felt it my duty as a gentleman to call on her and to explain that I did not give any cause for the rumors. And she was also very glad to see me, and she said that now, after I called on her and after the matter has been made clear between ourselves, she felt that she had more courage to deny all rumors."

While I was in the lawyer's private office he was called to the next room, which was a sort of reception room. Having nothing to do and without any intent or design, I glanced over his desk, which was strewn with papers. On top of a pile was a sheet of typewritten paper which was a carbon copy of a letter. I read:

> Mr. Morris Shulem, *Shadchen,*
> 421 Rivington Street, New York.
> Dear Mr. Shulem:
> I am a widow in a peculiar predicament. My husband used to smoke the K—— brand cigarettes and save the coupons. We needed two thousand coupons to get a cut-glass fern dish with artificial ferns, the kind that you never have to use water. Recently my poor husband died, leaving me a widow with only 994 coupons—

"Ah ha!" I said to myself. "Let him have his fun; now I'll have mine."

Three days later Mirmelstein called on me.

"Did you hear more rumors?" he asked.

"The latest rumors are that you and Miss Kanarik are secretly engaged to be married soon," I said. "The whole block is talking of your visit to Miss Kanarik."

"What can you advise me to do now?" Mirmelstein asked.

"Get married," I said. "Now I have a widow whose husband died and left her with 994 coupons of the K—— brand cigarettes and—"

"I don't care for widows!" he cut me off abruptly, blushing at the same time, for he understood that I suspected him.

"Excuse me," I apologized. "I was just joking. I would advise you only to go and see Miss Kanarik again. Maybe she can give you an advice what to do to offset the new rumor."

Mirmelstein hesitated a moment; then he said:

"I'll be honest with you, Mr. Shulem. I saw her many times already and we decided to let them talk, we do not care a bit at all. Because last night we decided that we would get married and invite the gossipers. Then what will they have to talk? So please send me a bill for being my *shadchen*."

34

Bercovich Takes Up Eugenics

"Mr. Shulem, are you going or coming?" was the greeting Joe gave me as I walked into Gonefsky's on a Tuesday late in the evening.

"What a question, Joe," I said.

What difference did it make if I was coming or going, as long as I stopped in for a glass of tea and a listen to 'what's news.'

"How would you like a fresh-baked poppyseed with your tea?" Joe asked.

Steady customers at Carol's restaurant understood the half-spoken menus and nodded approval, because you ate what the waiter brought to you anyhow.

"Mr. Shulem"—Joe always became confidential with me —"many a time I had made up my mind not to have any more dealings with that Bercovich, but every time he comes here he tells me such a hard-luck story, and he makes such

a face that I can't help pitying him, and I let him talk
to me.

"And this is one of his tricks. For as soon as you would
allow him to talk, he has you in his power. He has got
such a gift of a gab that it is impossible to argue with him.
If he were a drummer for a coffin factory, he could make
you buy your coffin on your wedding day. That's him, that
Bercovich the *shadchen!*

"How can I get rid of him? I don't want to get married
and if I do I must have lots of money."

"Yes," I said with sympathy. "Nowadays it is hard to get
married without money."

"Mr. Shulem, another glass of mild tea with lemon?"
inquired Joe. "All right I'll bring it. Bercovich said: 'It is
ten times harder to get married without money than without love, take it from me. It is only those slick fellows, the
eugenists, who know the trick how to arrange matches
without love or money. They have *mazel,* those eugenists.
He wished *shadchenics* was such a paying business as
eugenics.'

"Then Bercovich the *shadchen* told me a story that I
am sure will interest you.

"Some seven or eight years ago Bercovich, while solic-
iting business, met a young man, a poor law student. The
fellow was clever and handsome, just the thing for a rich
man who has a homely-looking daughter to get rid of. It
just happened that Bercovich had on his list a girl like that,
whose father was willing to give her $15,000, as she was
standing in the way of six younger sisters. Well, Bercovich
came up to that student and said: 'I have a girl for you with
$15,000 *mezumen,* not promissory notes.'

" 'What!' the young man angrily hollered. 'I sell myself
for money? Not on your life!'

" 'But look here, young man,' Bercovich said, 'don't be in

a hurry about making up your mind. If you will take a look at the girl you will see that whoever marries her will earn the money honestly.'

" 'I don't want to see her,' the young man said; 'and that is final.'

"That was seven or eight years ago. This week, Bercovich tells me, he met that same young man again. He is now a prosperous lawyer with an office in Nassau Street. Well, the first question Bercovich asked him was if he was already married.

" 'Married,' the lawyer replied.

" 'And you would not give me a show,' Bercovich reprimanded him.

" 'Well,' the lawyer said, 'I don't believe in *shadchens*.'

" 'Did you marry only for love alone, then?'

" 'No sir!'

" 'Aha, then you sold yourself for money, through another *shadchen*?'

"But Bercovich was too hasty in his conclusions.

" 'I married neither for love nor for money,' the lawyer explained. 'I married according to the advice of a professor of eugenics. My wife is neither young nor handsome. She was a widow with six children when I first met her, and she did not have a single penny in her possession. But I married her for the welfare of the human race. That's eugenics.'

"Then Bercovich said he would like to meet the lady and get some idea of the eugenic business, maybe he could learn it and go in it himself, as *shadchenics* is being played out.

"The lawyer laughed and said:

" 'Well, come to my house and have a bite with me.' It was supper time.

"On arriving at the lawyer's house Bercovich was introduced to the lawyer's wife. She was flat all around, an extremely tall woman and she had a face full of pimples and a wart was on the tip of her nose.

"And then Bercovich recognized her. It was the same woman that he had offered the lawyer eight years ago, but at that time she was younger and had $15,000, and she did not have six little ones hanging onto her apron strings. She had married meanwhile and had lost husband and money.

"Surely, the eugenists must be very clever if they could work up a job like that so smoothly. Bercovich says he is going to study eugenics. Maybe that will help him.

"Do you think it will, Mr. Shulem?" concluded Joe.

35

His Picture Bride

This story I am going to tell you is different. It is about a man who arrived three hours early for an appointment.

It is about Sam, who worked with Mr. Blitz in a wholesale jobbing business, and how it was arranged for him to meet Goldie. It was settled that Goldie was to come on the train from Stamford, Connecticut, and she was to be wearing a brown coat. Sam arrived at the Grand Central depot exactly three hours early, or about two hours before the train was scheduled to leave Stamford.

But Sam was there at the depot. He watched trains come and go. He watched people say good-by to one another and say hello to one another. With each arrival or departure of a train, Sam became more nervous.

Shulem, you're a little ahead of yourself.

To start from the beginning, it all happened at Mr. Blitz's daughter's engagement party, when I had the pleasure of being the *shadchen*. There I noticed a young man who, all evening, was sitting at the table and he did not take his eyes from a picture on the wall. He had a look. A faraway look. He hardly tasted anything from the sweet table, so, I finally filled up two glasses of wine and said to him:

"Here, my young man, have a drink with Shulem and banish all sad thoughts from your mind. Why worry? You are not being engaged tonight."

He laughed, taking the glass from me, and drank about half.

"Finish it," I said. "You act just like a *yente*. Drink it all and you will feel like a new man. Whatever Shulem the *shadchen* tells you to do, do it and you will never be sorry."

Then bending over a little, I ask him in a whisper:

"Tell me, do you like the girl on that picture?"

He blushed and that was sufficient, for I understood.

"Listen," I added, "I am willing to help you. I'm not surprised that you like her, for she does look pretty and sweet. But falling in love with a photograph is risky business."

My young friend became frightened, but I did not let him worry.

"Look here," I said, "I am going over to Mr. Blitz, our host, and ask who that girl is and how many years ago this photo was taken. Please, just have a little patience."

In a few minutes I had all the information. Yes, the photograph was of recent date, of a young girl, unmarried, and not even a steady. She was twenty-one and lived with her parents in Stamford, Connecticut.

The photograph was the picture of our host's niece, the youngest daughter of his only sister.

"Sam," Mr. Blitz addressed the young man, "I am sure Goldie will like you and when you see her you will find her more beautiful than her picture. She is a lovely girl, very bright, and a good housekeeper—not a loafer like most city girls."

We began to discuss how to arrange a meeting between the two people. Mr. Blitz proposed to write to his sister, acquainting her with the proposition, and we all agreed.

About two weeks passed in correspondence, and at last it is arranged that the girl should come on a Sunday morning, and to make the matter more romantic, Sam is to go and meet her at Grand Central and bring her over to her uncle's house in Brooklyn. And to make it more easy for Sam to recognize the girl in a Sunday crowd, it is arranged that Goldie should wear a brown coat.

By that time the girl had Sam's photograph and she liked him too.

So Sam was at the station three hours before Goldie's train was to arrive, trembling and his heart beating like a riveter.

And finally, there she was, and in a brown coat.

The minute he looked at her Sam turned on his heels and ran away. He ran straight for my house, and when I saw him I got frightened. I thought he became *meshugga*.

"You swindler! You crook!" he yelled at me, pounding his fist on the table.

"Calm yourself, young man," I said. "If you can prove that I am a swindler or a crook I'll give you a hundred dollars."

"I'll prove it right away!" he continued yelling. "That niece of Mr. Blitz is a woman of forty or forty-five, and not a girl of twenty-one, and she had a nose that looks like a *shofar*."

"And why are you so sure?" I asked. "Did she have a brown coat and come on the Stamford train?" Then I began to think that maybe after all that photograph was an old one.

"As sure as today is Sunday," he answered.

"I'll tell you," I said, "I'm going over to Blitz's house and see what he has to say. He is the man to be blamed. In two hours I will be back and we will talk."

At Blitz's house, everyone was glad to see me.

"What is the matter with Sam?" Mr. Blitz greeted me. "He didn't meet my niece at the depot. Did he back out?"

"He had a right," I said angrily. "It was not fair to fool him that way."

"Fool him? What do you mean?" Mr. Blitz wondered.

At this moment a pretty young girl came in from another room. She was like her picture on the wall.

"There must have been some misunderstanding," I said when I looked at the girl.

"I think so too," the girl answered. "I'm sure that I saw him at the station. I knew him by the photograph he sent me, but all of a sudden I saw him run away. I'm sure he ran before he could notice me."

"And that's all?" I asked.

"While I was standing there and wondering," the girl added, "I heard a woman cursing like a witch. I asked her what was the matter and she told me that she had just met a crazy man, who, on seeing her, took fright and ran away. 'I hope he breaks his neck running,' she said. 'Only in New York you meet such crazy people.' "

"Was there another woman in a brown coat on the same train with you?" I asked.

"Yes, that was the woman cursing," Goldie answered, "but she was a woman of at least forty-five, maybe older. He could not have taken her for me."

I could not help laughing.

That evening Sam was sitting in the parlor chatting and dancing to the radio music with Goldie. It was not a bad job after all.

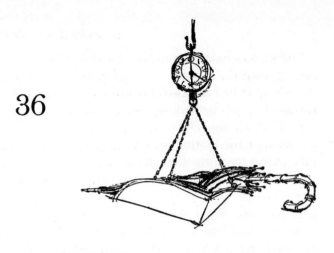

36

Farewell Rivington

Many times before have I said that Monday mornings are my time to think of a new *shidduch,* or to try and settle the *tzoris* of the world. Also, on Monday mornings, I'm not so sure, because of my profession, if I don't add a little to the *tzoris* of the world.

One such Monday morning I was sitting and thinking about shoemakers, and the saying about shoemakers' children going around with holes in their shoes. Many philosophers put much deep thinking in that saying—maybe because it has been with us for years and years. I can't put deep thinking in it because, to me, I feel the shoemakers are too busy making a living to support and feed their children. So what is there for deep thinking?

My wife, Minnie, however, has her own ideas about the shoemakers' children, and it usually comes out on a Monday morning after a Sunday night wedding that I *shadchened.* She will coyly open the conversation like this:

"Well, shoemaker, will you have time this week to take care of your own?"

That is Minnie's way of reminding me that we had two grown unmarried daughters, and what am I doing about it?

Fortunately, my girls have saved a small *nadan*, but they wanted to do their own picking and selecting. They are like the family that was in the retail ladies' ready-to-wear—the women of that family would buy their clothes elsewhere, and at retail, because they didn't like the style. So is it with my girls.

But Minnie and I were not too happy about our girls remaining single and after considerable *shmoos* between ourselves and Minnie's searching, we decided to say farewell to Rivington Street and move to Kelly Street, in the Bronx.

The Bronx is a fine section and Kelly a beautiful street, although, contrary to what the name would imply, there is not one Irishman on the block.

We—my wife, my two unmarried daughters and myself—were so tired the day we moved, that we went to bed early at night—about ten, I think. But as soon as I closed my eyes, my wife woke me up.

"Morris, the bell is ringing," she said. "Please go and see who is it."

The late visitor was a young man, a grocer. "I am very sorry to have disturbed your sleep," he apologized, "but I wanted to be ahead of my competitors and get your trade. I have the best herrings—real herrings, and smoked salmon, fresh bagels and rolls that are baked early every morning, and all the delights of the heart. And the stomach. I cater to the best families in the Bronx."

"You are very enterprising, indeed," I complimented him, "but as a rule I leave such matters to my wife. Come around tomorrow and see her."

He apologized again and left and I went back to bed.

Before I had time to fall asleep the bell rang again. I began to lose my patience, but had to run for the door and answer the ring before the ringing would awake my family.

"I know that Goldman was here before me," the second visitor said, "but I keep better merchandise and besides, I have a large family to support, while Goldman is a bachelor and is worth a lot of money."

"You don't say!" I exclaimed. "I did not know that."

"Well, it is good I told you about him. What shall I deliver for your breakfast? Rolls? Eggs? Butter? Fresh pot cheese?"

"You will have to come in the morning and see my wife about it," I told him.

He left, maybe a little disappointed, and I went back to bed, making up my mind not to open the door again, no matter how long the bell rings.

Some time passed. Maybe it was about a quarter past eleven when Minnie woke me up saying in a frightened voice:

"Morris, don't you hear somebody ringing? Answer the door or the bell is going to break."

I was out of bed again and already preparing a speech while walking to the door. When I opened it I found three men standing in the hallway.

"Nice time to ring a house bell!" I said. "And such ringing!"

"Well," one of the three men finally said, "every one of us was ringing for himself. We didn't think you were asleep already. Here in the Bronx we stay up late."

"Are you all grocers?" I asked.

"No," answered the same man. "I am the only grocer; this is Tony, the janitor, and this is the butcher who keeps his shop next to mine. We all came up to solicit your business."

"Tomorrow, gentlemen. Come tomorrow and see my wife about it. I never bother my head about housekeeping. Good night!"

"Morris," my wife said, as I told her who the visitors were, "now you go to sleep, and should anyone come again and ring the bell I will attend to him."

Right at that moment the bell rang. Minnie threw a shawl over her head and, opening the window, she called out:

"Are you a grocer, a baker, a butcher, or a milkman?"

"No," an anxious voice answered. "I must see your husband."

"Oh, you want the doctor," my wife surmised. "He lives next door to the right."

"What's the matter with you?"—and the anxious voice grew angry. "I want your husband, Morris Shulem the *shadchen*. I have traveled all the way from Central Park to Rivington Street, only to find that you moved to the Bronx, and now you send me to a doctor. What I need is a *shadchen,* and I need him right away. Now!"

It was a quarter of twelve when I admitted the stranger to my home.

"My name is Breitbard," he introduced himself. "It is maybe an unusual hour to call on a *shadchen*, but this is an unusual and urgent case. My daughter, who is one of the best girls in town, was to be married tonight, but the bridegroom failed to come and who knows what happened to him. I have a suspicion that at the last moment he changed his mind in favor of a widow with whom he has been keeping company when he lived in Baltimore. Now, Mr. Shulem, I must have a substitute."

"What do you mean?" I asked, for I was not sure if I understood him right. "Do you mean to say you want me to be a magician and at midnight I should wave a magic wand and give you another bridegroom?"

"I was told that you are one of the best *shadchens* in New York," he said with tears in his eyes, "and that you can do wonders. Have pity on my daughter; she will not be able to stand this disgrace. We have arranged for a catered wedding supper in the Arcadia Palace, with a good band, and we have invited many guests. Now they are all there in the Arcadia Palace, waiting and waiting. You are the only man in the world who can save my daughter."

"If I were you," I suggested, "I would go back to the hall and tell the guests to take their seats at the table and go ahead with the supper. You should also tell the musicians to play and the young people to start dancing. Turn your wedding into a good-riddance party. Your daughter should feel happy that she did not marry such a fickle-minded *goneff*. Your daughter did not lose a thing. And by marrying him she would have to regret all her life. Go and thank the good Lord for her *mazel*."

"All this is very sensible," Mr. Breitbard replied, "but good sense does not quiet people's talk. They would not believe we are sincere. The best thing, then, is still to get a substitute. Please look up your notebook for a young man who is of a decent family, making a fair living. If he has other qualities, that, of course, would be still better."

"And the *nadan?*" I asked.

"You bring the man, and I'll satisfy him," was the answer.

"I think I have it!" I said, a happy idea striking me. "You go back to Arcadia Palace and have your guests go ahead with the feast and merrymaking. I hope to be there very soon with good news."

It was a quarter past twelve when we both left my house. And we parted, Mr. Breitbard going toward his car, and I making my dash for Goldman's grocery.

The store was still open, with the lights burning low and Goldman counting the day's receipts. He was doing good business, I could see.

"I came to give you my breakfast order," I said, "for you made such a good impression on me that I could not fall asleep before I have given you a little business. Since I am a *shadchen* I was never so impressed by a young man as by you, tonight."

"Ninety-seven, ninety-eight, ninety-nine," he kept on, counting his money and talking to me at the same time. "I am glad to hear it, and you will be much more impressed by the quality of my smoked salmon, herrings—one hundred, hundred one, hundred two—"

"Business, business and business!" I criticized. "Have you nothing else in life but rolls and herrings? If you don't watch out you will become a pickled herring yourself. Get married and enjoy life!"

Then I told him of Mr. Breitbard's visit to my house.

"He is a fine citizen and his daughter is one grand girl," I said in conclusion. "Here is the chance of your life!"

You think I did not hook him? He was married that same night in Arcadia Palace.

When I returned home it was already near four in the morning. At seven I had to get up, and when I entered the hallway I found at my door eight large, bulky paper bags full of rolls, cream cheese, eggs, butter, all varieties of herrings and smoked salmon. To every bag was attached a bill, which bore the name of a different grocer. The bag which had no bill attached to it, of course, was delivered by Goldman.

A grocer cannot afford to have a honeymoon.

And when Minnie saw all the bags of groceries she said, "Well, Mr. Shoemaker, do you think you will have a chance to at least look at the children's shoes today?"

37

The Kabtzensohn Flat

For months after the big decision was reached that we should move, Minnie and my daughters commenced flat hunting. After something looked like a possibility, my ladies would *shlep* me to take a look. We wanted a flat, it should be on a nice street, it must be airy and close to transportation with good shopping.

Moving to a new apartment is an experience, an experience that I wouldn't wish on my worst enemy. Comes moving day there was even more excitement, such as:

"Where's the mover? He should have been here two hours ago?"

"Do you think he'll make it in one trip? Will he send a big truck?"

"He promised to do us first, now when he comes the helpers will be all tired out!"

And so on. . . .

It took us two weeks to say good-by to our old friends of the old neighborhood. Every evening, after we rented, we would talk about our new apartment and what we will find in the neighbors.

I said it's an experience to move? Let me tell you what happened to the Shulems.

If you are about to move to a new apartment, take my advice and find out if the former tenant has paid all his bills before moving out. I am giving you some valuable advice based on my own experience, and this isn't idle talk.

My troubles commenced the first week that I moved to the Bronx, and they kept on coming for two months following.

A few days after we moved in, a young man in a Palm Beach suit called, just at the time my wife, my unmarried daughters and I were eating our dinner. He carried a box of candy in one hand and a large bouquet of flowers in the other.

"Where is Frances?" he asked, looking a little surprised, without even saying 'Hello!'

"Frances?" Minnie repeated, staring at him.

"Yes, Miss Frances Kabtzensohn," answered the young man, "Mr. Jacob Kabtzensohn's daughter. They live here."

By this time I didn't know who was more annoyed, Minnie or the young man. We knew that a family by the name of Kabtzensohn had occupied our flat before we moved in; we found their name in the mail box. We finally convinced our caller that the Kabtzensohns had moved out.

"And she didn't even let me know where she moved," the visitor mused to himself. "Now I know that was not for me!"

The young man left and I saw no more of him, but I found his bouquet which he dropped in the hall. That,

I took into the house and presented to my wife with my compliments.

Three or four days after, another stranger came, and without introducing himself he said to me:

"I see by the name on your mail box that you have changed your name to Morris Shulem. But, Mr. Kabtzensohn, that will do you no good; you'll have to pay for that gold watch, or we'll be compelled to sue you."

"But who are you? A gold watch?" I asked. "I have never seen you before."

"Neither did I have the pleasure of meeting you," he replied. "I am the new collector for Price, Double & Co., and I have your record!"

"My record?" I asked.

"You took a $150 gold watch, promising to pay off at $10 per month, and you made only one payment," was the answer. "You are five months in arrears."

"Mr. Collector," I suggested, "you'd better go to the janitor or the grocer and find out whether I am Kabtzensohn or Shulem."

In less than five minutes the collector came back and apologized.

The week following we had calls from several more collectors. Of some we rid ourselves easily, while others were persistent and wanted proof that we had no connection with Mr. Kabtzensohn.

One day a young fellow who introduced himself to me as a "fixer" came and asked me how I stood with the police.

"I think you are looking for Mr. Kabtzensohn," I said. "He moved out some weeks ago. My name is Morris Shulem. I am a *shadchen* and I have nothing to do with the police."

"Well," the fixer said smiling, "if you think that you can fool the police by putting another name on your mail box you are very much mistaken. They are on to your game, and the sooner you'll let me fix the matter for you with the captain, the better it will be for your own safety."

"But for heaven's sake," I wanted to know, "tell me why should I fear the police?"

He laughed and said:

"Because you are running a gambling house."

When Minnie heard these words she came running from the kitchen, swinging a broomstick which she carried in both her hands, and began to belabor the fixer. He ran out and Minnie followed him until he was in the street.

"Bravo, Minnie," I applauded my wife, "tonight I'll take you to see the moving pictures. But, Minnie," I continued, when suddenly I was struck with a serious thought, "you know that fixer could be right; marriage is a gamble."

We both had a good laugh and we thought we were through with that fixer, but an hour later, as I was about to leave the house, two well-dressed men called. They looked around the living room, and one of them asked:

"Why is it so quiet here? Where are all the boys? Nothing happened, has it?"

"Gentlemen," I warned them, "you are in the house of Morris Shulem the *shadchen*."

"Who are you trying to kid," the other fellow said. "We know you, Mr. Kabtzensohn. Why are you afraid of us? You think we have no money? Here—" And he showed me a fat roll of bills.

At that moment I began to suspect that these two men were police detectives.

"Well, can't we have a game?" the other one asked.

"Not before I have fixed the police," was my answer.

"How are you going to do it?" they asked. "And why are you laughing? Tell us, what is the joke?"

"It is a joke," and I told them the whole story of my

troubles since I moved in my new home, in Kelly Street, in the Bronx.

"We are sorry, very sorry for having troubled you," one of the men said, "but we have been informed by the telephone less than an hour ago that Kabtzensohn's gambling joint had resumed business, but under new management. If we get hold of that guy who calls himself a fixer, we'll take care of him. I'm almost positive it was the same fellow who telephoned the complaint against you."

"Minnie," I asked my wife after the two detectives had left, "did you try to find out from the janitor what sort of a man was that Kabtzensohn, anyhow?"

"The janitor wouldn't tell," Minnie replied, "and I guess he has good reasons for not telling. But the neighbors told me that he was a gambler, and that his daughter helped him in his business, but his wife did not live with him."

One thing I am always sure, when Minnie gets information, it is reliable and complete. "My goodness," I said finally, "and we have to suffer for his sins!"

But that's not all!

Next morning, as I left the house to go downtown, a man who was standing outside, just in front of my door, approached me, saying, "I have a warrant for you. Come on!"

"A warrant for what?" I asked, feeling weak in my legs.

"For nonsupport. You failed to support your wife," the man of the law explained.

"Why," I protested, "my wife is right here in this house and I am supporting as best as I can."

"All right," the man replied. "You'll tell that to the judge and he'll change the charge to bigamy. Come on, Mr. Kabtzensohn!"

"But I am not Kabtzensohn," I argued, taking out some letters that I had in my pocket. "Look here."

"Don't you live on the first floor?" the officer asked.

"I do, but I am here only for the last sixteen days," I said. "The man you are looking for has gone about six weeks ago."

I had to be identified again by the janitor before the man with the warrant would let me go.

"I hope this will be our last trouble," Minnie prayed when I told her how I was about to be taken to court on a charge of neglecting a wife.

But it was not our last trouble. There was more ahead.

One night last week, as all of my family were already in their beds and I was sitting in the little room at the end of the hall, where I had my new little private office, I heard someone putting a key in the front door keyhole. I got very much scared, thinking it was a burglar, and before I could recover from my shock the door opened and a young man carrying two heavy suitcases entered.

As soon as I saw that the suitcases were loaded, my fear left me. Burglars do not carry heavy stuffed suitcases when they go on business.

"I am back from the South," the late visitor announced as he put down his baggage. "Well, how is Frances? Why didn't she write to me all the time I was away? But, say—"

He stopped abrubtly when he saw my face in the light. For a moment he stood still and grew pale, staring at me. When he recovered himself he inquired:

"What are you doing in my room?"

"May I ask with whom I have the honor to get acquainted at this hour of the night?" I wanted to know.

"I'm Sidney Goilem, Miss Kabtzensohn's intended," he explained, "we are to be married soon and this is my room. I boarded with the Kabtzensohns all the time that they lived in this house."

"But they moved out," I said, "and nobody knows where to."

"The robbers! They owe me $460!" the young man moaned. "I loaned them that amount in cash. Where shall I go now?"

I pitied him, for now he looked a little foolish, but kind. "Suppose," I said, "you stay here in your room for the night? Tomorrow I may move my office to the parlor and let you stay here as long as you want."

Minnie was willing to let Mr. Goilem board with us. "Maybe," she whispered in my ears, "he'll fall in love with one of our daughters."

Glossary

aleihem hasholem	peace to their memory
bar mitzvah	confirmation
boychakal	youngster
bubba monsis	old wives' tales
bubbie	grandmother, old woman
buchor	boy
choson	bridegroom
chupah	marriage canopy
eppis	something
essen	eat
fresser	glutton
gefillte (fish)	chopped fish
gesheft	business
gevalt	alarm
goneff	thief
kalle	bride
kapoot	done with
kibitzer	joker
kibitzarnie	headquarters for literati
kitke	twisted bread loaf
klop	beat
landsleite	home folks
landsman	compatriot
mach a tzimis	make a fuss
machuton; machutonim (pl.)	relation by marriage
marinierte (herring)	marinated, pickled

mazel	luck, fortune
mazel tov	good luck to you
meshugga (adj.)	crazy
meshugaas (**noun**)	insanity
mishpocho	relatives
momzer	scoundrel
nadan	dowry
nebich	poor fellow
nu	so
oleho hasholem	peace to her memory
olov hasholem	peace to his memory
Rosh Hashonah	Jewish New Year
schnorrer	beggar
Shabbos	Sabbath
shadchen	matchmaker
shidduch	marriage match
shlemiel	unlucky or clumsy fellow
shlep	carry, drag
shlimazel	same as *shlemiel;* bad luck
shmeer	flatter
shmoos	friendly chat
shmutz	dirt
shofar	ram's horn
shsha	silence, be quiet
shtuss	fuss
shtrudel	pastry
teiglech	bread and nut patties
tzoris	trouble
yente	old-fashioned woman